USA TODAY BESTSELLING AUTHOR

RACHAEL BLOOME

THE UNBOUND BOOKSHOP

a *Blessings Bay* N O V E L

For film and TV rights: hello@rachaelbloome.com

Cover Design: Ana Grigoriu-Voicu with Books-Design.

Editing: Krista Dapkey

Proofing: Beth Attwood

Series Reading Order

BLESSINGS ON STATE STREET

THE UNEXPECTED INN

THE UNBOUND BOOKSHOP

THE UNCOMPLICATED CAFÉ

THE UNINTENTIONAL TEAHOUSE

Lynn,

For supporting me from the beginning.
You're the best bonus mom and unofficial publicist a girl could
ever ask for

Letter From the Author

Dear Friend,

As a writer and reader, I love living vicariously through fictional characters. Occasionally, I even wish I could become a certain character and spend a day (or a dozen!) in their shoes.

That wish has never been stronger than when I wrote Sage Harper, thanks to her fanciful idea to open a floating bookstore. I frequently found my mind drifting into fantasy land, daydreaming about gorgeous vintage sailboats, books galore, and stunning sunset cruises across crystal waters. There is something so romantic and magical about the idea, and I hope you enjoy daydreaming about The Unbound Bookshop as much as I did while writing this story.

Have you ever wanted to step into the shoes of a beloved character? I'd love to hear about it. You can reach me at hello@rachaelbloome.com, 2945 Hwy 49 S, Mariposa, CA 95338, or in my private Facebook group, Rachael Bloome's Secret Garden Book Club.

I look forward to hearing from you!

Blessings & Blooms,

Rachael Bloome

Special Bonus Offer

AS A SPECIAL THANK you to my readers, I've created an exclusive (and completely FREE) members-only area of my website called the Secret Garden Club. When you join, you'll receive access to a wealth of bonus content, including short stories, extra scenes, and more.

Oh, and did I mention FREE BOOKS?

Adding to the fun, the content is regularly updated, so you never know what goodies you'll find.

By joining, you'll also receive exclusive emails with writing updates, sneak peeks, sales, freebies, and giveaways.

I'd love to stay in touch. You can join here: www.rachael bloome.com/pages/secret-garden-club.

Chapter 1

ABBY

ABIGAIL PRESTON STARED at the sleek lines of the custom sailboat decorating the glossy auction house brochure, tuning out the raucous bidding war over a sterling silver thimble set. As she studied the photograph, tears stung her eyes like a wayward splash of lemon juice. Would the guilt ever wane?

"Did I miss it?" Sage Harper flounced onto the chair Abby had saved for her, pink-cheeked and breathless, her hair a mass of windswept honey-blond curls.

Her friend's arrival yanked Abby from her melancholy thoughts, snapping her surroundings into focus. The auctioneer, calling out bids with over-punctuated precision. The stiff wooden chair that left her backside numb. The scent of stale coffee in paper cups and antiques newly released from dusty attics. Each sight and sensation helped shove her self-reproach into the back of her mind.

"I think they're saving the sailboat for last." Abby tucked the brochure into her purse and switched the bid paddle from her left hand to her right, ignoring her clammy palms.

"Thank goodness." Sage's shoulders slumped with her heavy exhale. "I can't afford to miss this opportunity. It may be my last chance."

"I know the feeling." Abby offered her friend a shaky smile. Although her coveted auction item wouldn't change her life the same way Sage's would, she'd been searching for the antique Spode sugar bowl for months—the last remaining piece to complete her set.

As if reading her mind, Sage nodded toward the stage and whispered, "Do you think that's your sugar bowl?"

The mysterious auction item sat on a small table, cloaked in a black cloth the size of a handkerchief.

Good old Herman Chesterfield sure loved his theatrics. Too bad the auctioneer's assistant—his ninety-year-old mother, Mabel—didn't get the memo. Preparing the next item in the auction lineup, the spunky senior wheeled a gilded frame resting on a rickety antique easel toward the stage, abandoning it by the ramp to wait its turn.

Abby tensed. The large photograph of a vintage sailing schooner held her gaze against her will. The same photograph from the brochure. The same photograph that haunted her dreams.

"There it is," Sage breathed. "The answer to my problem. At least, I hope so. Isn't she beautiful?"

Abby heard Sage speaking but couldn't process the words. Her mind reeled backward in time to the day two fishermen discovered the sailboat shipwrecked on an island off the coast of Blessings Bay—to the first thought that had flashed in her mind.

Please don't let it be Sam Bailey's boat.

She shivered at the memory, shame slithering up her

spine. Her fears weren't founded in the painful possibility of recovering his remains but in the unlikely chance he'd be found alive.

What kind of foster mom was she? What kind of *person*? Her sweet eight-year-old son prayed nightly for his father's safe return. And even though his dad had been missing at sea for months, Max Bailey's faith never wavered. Not even once.

Each night, she bowed her head beside him, her prayers drenched in sincerity. She *wanted* Sam to be found, safe and sound. She wanted father and son to be reunited. Of course she did! She wasn't a monster.

Or was she? The second she'd heard the word *shipwreck*, her heart had betrayed her—had betrayed Max. At the miraculous possibility of his father's rescue—of Sam returning for Max—she'd wanted to cry. Not tears of joy or relief. Tears of grief.

She'd longed to be a mother, from the moment she held her first baby doll wrapped in a pink polka-dot swaddle. Even after discovering her late husband's infertility, she'd dreamt of adopting a child—a child who needed all the love she had to share.

When Max came into her life last Christmas, he fit so effortlessly. As if she'd had a Max-shaped hole in her heart all those years. She didn't want to lose him or the family they'd built together.

Only upon learning the recovered sailboat belonged to local legend and eccentric billionaire, Edwin Mackensie, not Sam Bailey, did the relief finally come.

And that had to make her the most selfish person in the world.

"Our next treasure may be my favorite of the day."

Herman broke through her thoughts. Standing tall in a tweed suit, he pinched the black cloth between his white-gloved fingertips. At some point during her self-chastising reverie, he'd moved on from the thimble set.

"While it's tragically been separated from its family, it's no less remarkable as a standalone piece." He overenunciated with the tiniest hint of an English accent. An accent the self-proclaimed anglophile had acquired purely from binge-watching British television. "This exquisite, early nineteenth century, bone china sugar bowl by the irrefutably flawless Great Britain–based houseware company, Spode, would be a coup for any serious collector." He whipped the cloth away with the dramatic flourish of a matador, eliciting oohs and aahs from the crowd.

"This is it." Sage gave her hand a quick squeeze.

Abby squeezed back, grateful for the moral support. *Time to focus.*

"The gold edging is pristine," Herman continued. "And the delicate floral design featuring blue and purple violets is hand-painted, making this piece one of a kind."

"He's laying it on a little thick, isn't he?" Sage whispered.

Abby scooted toward the edge of her seat, her heart thrumming. She'd counted on not many people coveting a single sugar bowl. Didn't most collectors prefer complete sets? But the way Herman went on and on about it, she might have more competition than she'd anticipated.

"Let's start the bidding at a mere fifty dollars."

"Fifty dollars?" Sage hissed. "For one sugar bowl?"

Abby raised her paddle.

"We have fifty. Do we have sixty?"

Abby held her breath as Herman scanned the multipurpose town hall turned temporary auction house. Since Herman only held these events biannually, there wasn't an empty seat to be found. Somewhere, in the shoulder-to-shoulder throng, another paddle shot into the air.

"We have sixty," Herman recounted. "Do we have seventy?"

Abby lifted her paddle, her pulse pounding in her ears.

The same bidder countered, but her contender remained hidden behind a trio of women wearing enormous floral-rimmed sun hats.

She sat a little straighter, reaching her hand higher in the air, as if elevation would somehow grant her an advantage. No such luck. Her opponent pounced before she'd even had a chance to lower her arm.

For the next several minutes, they played an unrelenting round of ping-pong, lobbing bids back and forth until the price rocketed to $150. At this rate, she'd blow through her entire budget in mere seconds.

"I don't know how much longer I can do this," Abby confessed in a hoarse whisper. "I brought two hundred, but hadn't expected to pay anything close to that amount." She slid the bills from her back pocket, splaying them between her fingers to see if they'd miraculously multiplied.

"Two hundred for a sugar bowl?" Sage matched her hushed tone. "Are you sure you need it that badly?"

Abby swallowed against the uncomfortable dryness in her throat. Did she *need* it? Not exactly. But from the moment she'd opened her boutique inn a few months ago, she'd longed to complete the set. And now that she'd booked her first bigwig guest at Blessings on State Street, she had even more motivation.

Sadie Hamilton—the fiancée of billionaire philanthropist Landon Morris—had reserved her brand-new Blessings & Blooms package for herself and her maid of honor. The friend also happened to be famous, and her lifestyle YouTube channel, Grow with Lucy Gardener, had recently received praise on a national talk show.

Upon checking in later that week, the two women would enjoy four days of pampering, relaxation, and luxury, starting with a traditional afternoon tea. Abby had her heart set on using her vintage Spode tea set but couldn't bring herself to substitute a mismatched sugar bowl. Not when Lucy Gardener would be filming every infinitesimal detail of their stay.

After a career ghostwriting cookbooks, making other people's visions come to life, the inn was the first endeavor to bear her own name. The first undertaking that represented her own accomplishments, her own dreams. She had to get it right.

Of course, there was always a slim chance she'd chosen to fixate on an external goal like buying the sugar bowl to avoid processing her conflicted emotions about Max, but that was an issue for another day.

Before she knew what she was doing, she heard herself say, "Two hundred dollars."

"Two hundred dollars," Herman repeated with an expression of equal parts surprise and delight splashed across his sharp, angular features.

A collective hush settled around the room, except for the squeak of folding chairs as everyone turned to glance in her direction.

Heat swept up her neck. What had she done? She had no

business spending a small fortune on something so frivolous. Max outgrew his clothes every other day, and even with the stipend she received from the state as a foster mom, raising a rapidly growing boy cost more than she'd ever imagined. Plus, what would Logan think?

Her blush deepened. They'd only been dating a few months, but she already factored her beau/business partner into most areas of her life. Between running the inn and raising Max, they made the majority of their decisions together. Would he understand her impulsive purchase?

With every muscle now knotted and tense, Abby craned her neck to see around the row of derby hat-adorned women who'd thankfully shifted in their seats to gawk at her.

Her breath hitched the second she glimpsed her competition. Archie Higgins, the octogenarian owner of the local grocery store, clumsily tapped a cell phone screen—a cell phone he clearly didn't know how to use.

What on earth did a widower who considered heavy-duty paper plates fancy dinnerware want with an antique sugar bowl?

To her horror, Archie set down the phone and raised his paddle.

"There you have it, ladies and gentlemen," Herman remarked with unbridled glee. "The current bid is $210. Do I hear two-twenty?" He twisted the end of his petite handlebar mustache, gazing at her expectantly.

Her heart stopped. Archie had outbid her. For a sugar bowl. It didn't make sense.

For a millisecond, her thoughts flickered to the money sitting in the bank—the money she hadn't touched since her husband, Donnie, died over a year ago. Maybe she could ask

Sage for a short-term loan and— *No*. She gave a sharp shake of her head, dismissing the unconscionable idea. She couldn't use that money. Not even for this.

With painful resignation, she set the paddle in her lap, admitting defeat.

"Two hundred and ten dollars going once, going twice, and sold, to the tea lover in the denim overalls," Herman announced with unnecessary theatrics since everyone in the room knew Archie by name.

The one thing Abby felt confident everyone *didn't* know about Archie was why he'd taken a sudden and expensive interest in fine china.

Chapter 2

LOGAN

Two hundred and ten dollars?

Logan Mathews gawked at his cell phone screen. He'd just given Archie Higgins permission to spend beaucoup bucks on a sugar bowl. A sugar bowl! Had he lost his mind?

Okay, so it wasn't just *any* sugar bowl. It was *the* sugar bowl. The one Abby had been hunting for months. She'd been talking about throwing some sort of fancy-schmancy tea party for their guests at the inn, and for some reason, the miniature bowl with a matching lid played a critical role. He didn't understand the details, but the instant Abby saw it listed on Herman's auction brochure, she hadn't stopped gushing about it. Which gave him an idea.

In hindsight, likely a very *bad* idea.

He set his phone on the white quartz countertop, face-up, so he'd see Archie's next text the second it came through, and went back to work slapping labels on small glass jars. The scent of frou-frou rash balm filled the kitchen with hints of coconut, mint, and lime, but Logan barely noticed.

There's no way the bid price could go any higher, right? How many people wanted an old sugar bowl?

Logan shot another glance at his phone. *Nothing.* Anxiety vibrated through his body like an idling jet engine. He'd counted on spending fifty or sixty bucks. Maybe seventy-five. But this was wild. Was Abby the one upping the bid so high?

He groaned, regret slamming against his chest. What kind of genius thought it was romantic to bid against his own girlfriend? Granted, his last relationship had bombed eons ago, and he was out of practice in the romance department. But he didn't think he was *this* rusty. He could hear his old Air Force buddies now. *Way to go, Nugget. You rolled in with your hair on fire and overshot the target.*

"Hey, twitchy fingers. It's upside down." Evan Blake's teasing tone broke through his thoughts.

Logan blinked, redirecting his attention to the jar clasped in his hands. The words *Evan Blake's Epic Rash Balm* stared up at him, but backward. *Drat.*

"Sorry, man. I was distracted." He carefully peeled off the label and reapplied it right side up.

"Yeah, no kidding." Evan chuckled. "What's up?" He set a fresh batch of newly filled jars on the counter.

"Waiting on a final word from Archie. And the anxiety might kill me." The erratic pulse and heart-hammering-in-your-throat sensations were all too familiar from his time flying an F-16, but somehow, this felt more intense.

"Oh, right. Today's the auction. How's that going?"

"Could be better. I'm already out over two hundo, and I'm just now realizing Abby might not appreciate being outbid."

"I think she'll forgive you once you give it to her and she sees what you put inside."

"Good point." Some of the pressure eased in Logan's chest. He sure hoped Evan was right.

"Who needs to forgive you and what for?" Evan's dad, Michael Blake, strolled into the kitchen clutching an enormous Tupperware container.

"Don't worry, Mr. B. Nothing nefarious." Logan sniffed the air. The perpetual scent of piña colada now carried a distinct whiff of cinnamon and spice.

"That's a relief. Then I can, in good conscience, offer you one of Bonnie's special cinnamon rolls." Mr. B peeled back the lid, releasing a rush of aromatic steam.

Logan's mouth watered. Bonnie Larsen sure knew how to bake.

"I gotta say, Dad"—Evan grabbed three plates from the cupboard—"as happy as I am that you and Bonnie are dating, all these snack breaks are bad for business."

"It's the price you pay for running Epic Inc. out of my kitchen," his dad teased.

"Touché." Evan flashed a lopsided grin.

Since Evan lived in a seashell-sized bungalow on the beach, his dad offered to let him run his new startup from his sprawling midcentury modern home. With its impressively detailed craftsmanship—including a seamless wall of windows overlooking the ocean that defied logic—and state-of-the-art fixtures, it was exactly the sort of place you'd expect from the owner of M.B. Construction. A little too modern for Logan's tastes. But then, he was hardly objective. Not even Buckingham Palace could compare to the inn he ran with Abby. She made Blessings on State Street paradise simply by being there, and he didn't care how sappy that sounded.

From the moment they met last Christmas, she'd completely changed his life. He'd gone from a self-proclaimed recluse to someone who not only left the house once in a while, but a guy who actually had friends. Friends like Evan, who'd offered him a part-time job when he'd needed a little extra cash. A job he enjoyed way more than he'd expected.

The tasks—jarring, labeling, packaging, and shipping—were rudimentary, but he got to work with Evan, listen to Motown as loud as he wanted, and, thanks to Bonnie, he ate like a king. Plus, the hours were flexible, which meant he could fit them in between his caretaker responsibilities at the inn and helping Abby with Max.

Mr. B handed them each a cinnamon roll. The plump mound of buttery goodness drenched in icing obscured most of the plate. Logan dug his fork into the soft, spongy dough, but paused midbite. "What are you guys doing?"

The father-son duo leaned against the opposite counter in the exact same position—right ankle crossed over their left, the plate held precisely at chest level. Side by side, they looked scary similar. As if they might be the same person, only one of them had traveled back in time thirty years. They had identical blond hair, blue-green eyes, and a small bump on the bridge of their nose. But that wasn't the spooky part. In perfect rhythm, they both scooped out the center of their cinnamon roll.

"We're eating," Evan mumbled past the massive bite in his mouth. "What's it look like?"

"I see that, Captain Obvious. But why'd you go straight for the center?"

"Why not?" Evan shrugged.

"Because it's weird."

"I didn't realize I'd broken proper pastry protocol," Evan joked. "Maybe I need to brush up on the handbook."

"I'll email you a copy," Logan lobbed back with a good-natured grin.

"You'll need to add an addendum for Bonnie's cinnamon rolls," Mr. B interjected. "She hides a creamy caramel in the middle of each one."

"Ah, I see. So, you eat the best part first instead of saving it for last like a normal person? That's definitely a code violation. I'll have to take it up with the review board."

"I'll shoulder the penalties on behalf of my son since he learned the bad habit from me," Mr. B offered, going along with the gag. "Sins of the father and whatnot."

"Thanks, Dad." Evan and his father shared a matching slanted smile.

As he watched the exchange, the hollow void in Logan's chest expanded—the aching cavern where memories of his father lived. Every nuanced detail remained cemented in his mind. The deep lines around his eyes and mouth. The small scar on his jaw, by his left ear where he'd cut himself shaving. He was only seven when his parents died, but he'd held on to the mental images as tightly as the rip cord on a parachute.

His father should be here now, to give him advice. His mother, too.

That's probably why he related so well to Max. He knew exactly how it felt to lose the two people closest to you. The two people who were supposed to help guide and protect you in a confusing, chaotic world.

The cinnamon roll forgotten, he stuffed his hand into the front pocket of his jeans, fingering the frayed edges of the tiny velvet bag—the one with his mother's ring. He still remembered the way she'd spritzed it with Windex whenever she cleaned the windows. The solitaire diamond was simple, but thanks to the Windex bath he'd given it that morning in her honor, it sparkled brighter than anything he'd ever seen.

His phone buzzed, and he yanked his hand from his pocket to check the text.

Two words appeared on screen.

Got it.

Relief rippled through him, followed by exhilaration. But the euphoria didn't last long.

An unsettling realization rammed into his brain, knocking the grin off his face.

"What happened?" Evan asked, noting his stricken expression. "You didn't win the bidding war?"

"I did, but—" Logan hesitated to admit the gaping hole in his plan. "I have a minor problem. I know I want to give Abby the engagement ring inside the sugar bowl, but I don't know how I should give Abby the *sugar bowl*. Do I wrap it? Tie a bow around it? Should I put sugar in it first? And what kind? The fancy little cubes? Or the regular granular stuff?"

Evan's eyes widened, and he looked equally stumped.

"Proposals don't have to be complicated." Mr. B offered his wise counsel while licking the icing off his fork.

"Not according to my ex." Logan snorted. Not only had his former fiancée, Kelli Clayton, picked out her own engagement ring, she'd told him exactly how to propose, down to the pair of shoes he should wear. The elaborate display took place at a popular Air Force event and involved a skywriter, fireworks, and a couple thousand of their closest friends.

Mr. B set his empty plate in the sink. "The key is keeping her interests in mind. What's important to Abby?"

"Max. The inn. Her friends." Logan rattled off the list without any reservation.

"Great. Then whatever you do, make sure it includes those elements, and you'll do just fine."

"Does that give you any ideas?" Evan asked.

"Yeah, actually. It does." As the plan coalesced in his mind, he said a silent prayer for the one detail he couldn't control.

Abby's answer.

SAGE

THE AUCTION HOUSE buzzed with surprise over Archie's unexpected win.

Sage Harper swiveled in her seat to face her friend, feeling her loss almost as acutely as if it had been her own. "I'm so sorry, Abby. I really thought you'd win."

Abby managed a small smile. "It's okay. I guess Archie needed it more. Maybe it reminds him of his wife?"

Sage returned her smile, in awe of her selfless attitude. Abby had to be the kindest, most gracious person she'd ever met. Somehow, she managed to wish even her competitors well. While Sage stopped short of desiring *harm* against her rivals—most notably the indomitable Mrs. Cordelia Cahill— she didn't exactly wish them *well*.

"And now," Herman bellowed theatrically, as if tasked with introducing the Queen of England herself, "the moment you've all been waiting for."

Sage inched forward, her toes nervously tapping the hardwood floor, then stopped herself as her grandma Shirley's soothing voice slipped into her thoughts. *Stress kills more people than cigarettes.* Sage had no clue if the claim had merit, but Grandma Shirley believed it adamantly enough for the both of them. If Sage so much as drummed her fingernails, Gran would whip out the dried lavender satchels and chamomile tea.

As Herman's mother rolled the easel on stage one centimeter at a time, Sage inhaled and exhaled slowly, mimicking the deep-breathing exercise from Gran's daily yoga class. So what if her entire future relied on winning this auction?

"Don't worry." Abby placed a reassuring hand on her arm. "If you don't get this boat, another one will come along."

"Thanks." Sage forced a smile and refrained from pointing out the obvious—she couldn't afford most boats on the market. She had fifteen thousand dollars to her name, and the kind of boat she needed usually sold for upward of fifty thousand. Sometimes even *hundreds* of thousands.

Her single ounce of hope came by way of Verna Hoffstetter—a one-woman rumor mill—who'd confided that the boat on today's auction block had a ridiculously low starting bid. And only a few people in town had expressed interest in the fixer-upper.

Herman flipped through his little leather-bound notebook, mouthing a few silent words like a keynote speaker preparing for their speech.

Abby leaned in, lowering her voice further. "For what it's worth, I want you to win this boat even more than I wanted the sugar bowl. Someone needs to go toe-to-toe with Cordelia Cahill. She's been untouchable for far too long, from what I've heard."

The familiar fire of frustration burned in Sage's chest.

Cordelia thought she was so clever when she opened The Best of Times, a bookstore that only sold *New York Times* best sellers. But the limited selection had been a sore spot among locals for years. Especially since Cordelia wouldn't even special order a book that hadn't made the exclusive list. Everyone knew she only stayed in business thanks to her husband's deep pockets.

To make matters worse, due to a centuries-old noncompete bylaw, no one else could open a bookstore in town. A bylaw Cordelia had delighted in recounting when Sage recently presented her business plan before the town council.

This wasn't the only occasion one of the Cahills had trampled on Sage's dreams—or her heart. But this time, she'd fight back. Even if it meant buying a sailboat despite her complicated history with the seafaring vessels. Hopefully this foray would have a happier ending.

"Thanks." She squeezed Abby's hand, attempting to absorb some of her optimism. "Let's hope no one else wants a dilapidated sailboat that's been shipwrecked on a deserted island for months."

Herman snapped his notebook shut, signaling the bidding war for the sailboat was about to begin.

Sage inhaled another yogic breath.

This was it. Her Hail Mary. The best—and arguably *only* —chance she had at fulfilling her childhood dream.

This was her loophole. The bylaw only applied to businesses founded on Blessings Bay *soil*. But a floating bookstore? That was fair game.

Herman faced the crowd, his features reverent and austere. *Sheesh*. Was the man hosting an auction in Blessings Bay or performing *Hamlet* on Broadway?

"Ladies and gentlemen." He addressed the crowd with a sweeping hand. "Allow me to paint you a picture. One of romance and adventure. Heartache and rebirth."

Despite his overcooked performance, Sage found herself enraptured—along with everyone else in the room—as Herman shared the boat's colorful history. He began with how the quirky billionaire owner, Edwin Mackensie, had it built for his late wife, Mira, on their silver anniversary, and ended with her tragic death last year.

"As she slipped into that good night," Herman recounted with solemn veneration, clutching the bow tie at his throat, "so did her beloved sailboat. The *Marvelous Mira*, as it was christened, languished at the Blessings Marina, forever moored in sweet sorrow, until a storm broke its tethers, casting it out to sea to be reborn among the waves. It's that rebirth it hopes to find today."

"And I thought he was hamming it up with the sugar bowl," Abby whispered.

Sage cleared the emotion from her throat. She didn't usually buy into Herman's histrionics, but all his melodramatic rambling about rebirth had struck a nerve. That's exactly what she needed—rebirth. She'd been languishing at her own proverbial moor. The moor of meandering part-time jobs and morose indecision. She needed a fresh start. To finally find her purpose.

"When you look at this custom-built forty-five-foot sailing schooner," Herman continued, "you may see peeling paint and weathered sails. But if you look closer, you'll see the wind and waves, calling you to a new life. A better life. A—"

"Five thousand dollars!" Sage shouted before he'd had a

chance to finish his spiel. She immediately slapped a hand over her mouth, embarrassed by her impulsive outburst. What had come over her?

Herman frowned, visibly irked by the interruption.

"Sorry." Her cheeks flushed. "Please, continue."

He expelled a short sigh that sounded both pious and pointedly resigned. "Never mind. We might as well begin. We have a starting bid of five thousand. Do I hear six?"

Several paddles shot into the air, and Sage's heart sank. *Thanks a lot, Herman, for the Shakespearean-level sales pitch.*

Before she could blink twice, the price rocketed from five thousand to thirteen. How high could she go? She had fifteen, but she'd need money for repairs. And *food*.

"I have thirteen thousand," Herman repeated. "Do I hear fourteen?"

Eh. Who needed to eat, anyway? Sage raised her paddle.

"Fourteen," Herman called out, nodding in her direction. "Do I hear fifteen?"

Sage scooted toward the edge of her seat, dizzy with desperation. A second passed. Then another. Her pulse hummed in her ears.

"Fourteen, going once," Herman sang like sweet, sweet music. Tears of joy and relief pricked her eyes. "Going twice." He raised his gavel, and a zing of electricity coursed through her. In a matter of seconds, everything would change. She could finally look at her life with a sense of pride, not self-pity. She could finally let go of the past. She could—

"Twenty-five thousand," a deep, commanding voice cut across the room.

Herman gawked, and a collective gasp whooshed through the air.

Sage's stomach lurched into her rib cage, colliding with her heart.

Please, no. It can't be. Not him. Not after all these years.

All eyes turned toward the back, eager to put a face to the eleventh-hour bidder.

But Sage didn't have to look. She knew each intonation —the rhythm, pitch, and timbre—by memory.

No matter how hard she tried to forget.

Chapter 4

FLYNN

FLYNN CAHILL STOOD unfazed by the sea of prying eyes and unapologetic whispers. As an identical twin in one of the town's most prominent families, he'd grown accustomed to unwanted attention. Unwanted attention that had only increased the day his brother, Kevin, died—one of the many reasons he hadn't been back to Blessings Bay in years, despite it being the most beautiful, idyllic place on the planet. And thanks to his globe-trotting job with the family business, he'd traveled to enough countries to compare.

"Twenty-five thousand?" Herman uttered more as a question than a statement.

"Yep. Unless the other bidder would like to counter." Flynn slipped one hand in the front pocket of his suit pants. He'd learned the trick watching his father handle business negotiations from as far back as his toddler years. *You want to look casual and unconcerned,* his dad had instructed while three-year-old Flynn had pretended to take notes on his fully functioning laptop. *Like you couldn't care less. Your apparent indifference will rattle your rivals, giving you the advantage.*

Herman glanced at someone seated in the center of the crowd.

Flynn shifted his stance to peer around a tall gentleman blocking his view, then instantly regretted the move. The split-second glimpse of his competitor slashed a knife through his heart.

He hadn't seen Sage Harper in almost ten years. Not since his brother's funeral. He flinched at the painful memory threatening to bob to the surface.

Despite the decade-long lapse since their last interaction, he could still close his eyes and mentally trace each curve of her satin-soft tendrils. He could still breathe in her hair's sweet, haunting scent of lavender and wildflower honey. A single whiff used to drive him crazy.

He shook away the unwelcome thought, mirroring Sage's own shake of her head, announcing her defeat. At the motion, her curls bounced from side to side, taunting him.

But he'd won. He could check off another item on his brother's bucket list—the bucket list he'd promised to complete, no matter the personal cost.

And yet, despite his victory, a heavy weight settled in his stomach like an anchor burdened with regret. Regret he'd never escape. Regret he deserved to carry for the rest of his life.

The room reverberated with hushed rumblings, and he could almost see the gossip column being written in real time.

After ruthlessly abandoning his longtime girlfriend without so much as a goodbye, Flynn Cahill is back in town to break her heart, yet again.

"And there we have it." Herman lifted his gavel, yanking

Flynn's thoughts from his fictitious headline. "Twenty-five thousand, going once. Going twice."

Flynn braced himself for the bang of the gavel—a sound that would now be bittersweet. Why did his competition have to be Sage, of all people? Didn't they already have enough emotional baggage surrounding sailboats?

"And sol—" Herman's hand froze midair when someone at the front of the room loudly cleared their throat.

Flynn couldn't make out the person's identity behind a wall of frilly oversize hats, but he secretly wanted to thank the interrupter for stalling. He needed more time to figure out his next move. Giving up the boat wasn't an option. He owed it to his brother. But he didn't want to hurt Sage. Not again.

What other choice did he have?

Herman stepped off the stage and stooped, his palm cupped to his ear, presumably to make out what this mysterious person was saying.

Herman's eyes widened, then he nodded, bobbing his head of silver-streaked hair. With a dazed expression, he padded back to the stage.

Flynn's pulse raced, picking up speed with each step Herman took.

Okay. Time's up. What are you going to do?

How many times had he watched his dad make the tough calls, unflinching? How many times had his father chastised him for lacking the killer instinct? He'd spent his entire adult life trying to measure up—to fill his perfect brother's shoes. He couldn't wimp out now.

"Well, ladies and gentlemen," Herman said slowly, "we've had a rather unorthodox turn of events."

A chair squeaked, and someone in the front row stood. *What in the world?* Flynn did a double take, dumbfounded. The man wore a three-piece suit, felt fedora, oversize sunglasses, and a long silk scarf wrapped around his neck, partially covering his face. The quirky dresser had to be Mackensie. The guy had a flair for the unusual.

More whispers and murmurs skittered through the air.

Flynn fixed his gaze on Herman, his teeth gritted. *Come on. Let's get this over with already.*

"I'm afraid this concludes today's auction." Herman rapped his gavel on the podium. "Thank you for attending. Please see my assistant, Mabel, to collect your items."

"Wait a minute," Flynn called out as townspeople scrambled from their seats. "What about my sailboat?"

The second the words left his mouth, he felt Sage's glare bore through him. *Welp.* If he had any doubts before, they were gone now. She definitely still hated him. Probably even more than before, now that he'd outbid her. Could he blame her?

He'd thought about calling her over the years, to try to explain, to apologize. But how could he tell her the truth? *No way.* He couldn't cross that bridge. Not then. Not now. Not ever.

Even if it meant she'd loathe him forever, he couldn't tell her what really happened that night.

The night his brother died.

It suddenly felt like a large stone had wedged in his throat. He tried to swallow, but strangely, had forgotten how.

Wait. Was Herman talking to him?

"If you and Miss Harper would please join me in the back office for a bit more privacy."

"Me?" she asked, as if there was another woman named Sage Harper. As if there could ever be another woman in the world like her.

"Yes, mademoiselle." Herman turned to him and added with the same ridiculous formality, "Monsieur, if you'd please follow me."

The guy wasn't French. Or British, for that matter. But at this moment, Flynn didn't care. Herman could speak to him in Pig Latin as long as the words translated to *Here's the title to your new boat.* He had to get out of there—and away from Sage—as soon as possible. The longer he stayed in her presence, the more disoriented he felt. He'd actually forgotten how to *swallow.* He couldn't get more pathetic than that.

Flynn gestured for Sage to go first, and gave her a wide berth, following several steps behind, averting his gaze. But not before he noticed she still wore the braided friendship bracelet around her ankle. The one she'd made for each of them—him, Kev, and herself—the summer before his brother died.

The sight of the faded blue and white thread tied his stomach tighter than a bowline knot.

Focus, Flynn. Don't be weak. He heard his father's voice in his ears and straightened his shoulders.

Herman led them into a cramped shared office space with an antique desk, filing cabinets, and matching brocade armchairs. He motioned for them to sit, but they both declined.

Let's hurry this along.

Sage stood against the far wall, arms crossed, with the expression of a feral cat surrounded by slowly rising water.

One wrong move and she might claw his eyes out, which he admittedly deserved.

He tried not to notice the way sunlight streamed from the small window, outlining her perfect figure with an amber glow.

Get a grip, buddy. Even bathed in anger and apprehension, his ex had never looked more beautiful. Way more beautiful than would be wise to admit, even to himself.

He swallowed against the uncomfortable roughness coating his throat, trying his hardest to concentrate. "What's going on, Herman? I won the bid, fair and square."

"I understand, monsieur. But the boat's owner, Edwin Mackensie, has pulled it from the auction."

"What?" Sage cried. "Why?"

"He'd like to make you both a proposition," Herman explained.

"I don't understand." Sage said what he was thinking. "What exactly is going on here?"

"It's hard to explain." Herman shifted his feet, visibly uneasy. "You know how Mr. Mackensie is."

"A few sails short of seaworthy?" Flynn teased, then winced. His father's voice broke through his thoughts again, ever the critical conscience. *No jokes. No wisecracks. It's time to grow up or no one will take you seriously.* "No disrespect. I only meant he has some oddities."

"He's a bit eccentric, yes," Herman agreed. "But it may be to your advantage this time. At least, for *one* of you," he said with a melodramatic flourish. "He'd like you to locate something on board the sailboat. Something he'd given up hope of ever finding."

Flynn cast a quick glance at Sage, but she didn't appear to have a clue, either.

"It's his late wife's diary," Herman explained. "She wrote in it religiously whenever she set sail but kept it hidden from the crew. Mr. Mackensie has hired countless people to locate it, since he won't board the boat himself, but all attempts have failed."

"What makes him think we'll have more success than everyone else?" Sage asked.

"He wants you to live aboard the boat for three days—safely docked at the marina, of course—fully immersing yourselves in every nook and cranny. Whoever finds the diary can keep the boat for the impossibly low price of five thousand dollars."

"Five thousand dollars?" Sage breathed, her eyes sparkling. Her entire posture had shifted from closed off to adorably eager.

Flynn couldn't look away. This was the Sage he remembered. Vibrant. Hopeful. Earnest. For one irrational moment, he actually relished the possibility of being trapped together—to recapture even one second of what they'd lost. But he couldn't step foot on a sailboat. And definitely not with Sage. Not after—he forcibly shoved the thought aside with a sharp breath.

Don't even go there.

"That's correct," Herman confirmed, assuaging Sage's disbelief. "If you agree to the terms, I'll draw up a quick contract. You have forty-eight hours to prepare yourself for boarding the—"

"Hold on," Flynn interjected. "This doesn't sound nuts to anyone else? Why three days? Why us? Why now?"

"I've learned not to question Mr. Mackensie's idiosyncrasies," Herman admitted. "His actions may not make sense at first, but there's always a method to his madness."

Madness being the operative word, Flynn thought. "And what if I find the diary on day one?"

"What if *you* find it?" Sage wore her glare again. *Good grief.* Even irritated, with her face all scrunched up, she looked gorgeous.

Focus, Flynn. "Or if *you* do," he said, getting back on track. "Whatever. It doesn't matter. My question is hypothetical. If one of us finds the diary on the first day, do we have to fulfill the full seventy-two hours on board?"

"Yes, that would be the arrangement."

"Wait a minute," Sage said slowly, as if a crucial piece of the puzzle had just clicked into place. "Three days. On board the sailboat. *Together?*"

"That is accurate, yes."

"I'm sorry. I can't do it." From the look of horror on her face, you'd think he'd proposed sharing a prison cell with a psychopath.

"I understand, mademoiselle. And if you'd like the boat to go to Mr. Cahill by default—"

"Wait." Sage closed her eyes and drew in a deep breath before opening them again, her expression resigned. "Fine. I'll do it. Under one condition."

"And what might that be?" Herman asked.

"The boat is forty-five feet long. And I expect Mr. Cahill to stay as far away from me as possible."

Her words stung like salt water slapping a wound, but he nodded. "Works for me."

Putting distance between them would be in his best interest, too.

In fact, it may be the only way he'd survive.

Chapter 5

LOGAN

COME ON, come on, come on.

Logan wasn't sure he'd survive another second of suspense. Waiting for the right minute to propose should be added to the categories of cruel and unusual punishment.

He lingered in the doorway between the kitchen and dining room, cradling a towering platter of fresh-from-the-oven scones. He hadn't eaten a single crumb all morning, but not even the rich, buttery scent of pastries could divert his attention from the day's mission.

Abby flitted around the long antique table, readjusting a rosebud here, a cucumber sandwich there, while Max and several of Abby's friends sat in tall high-backed chairs, waiting for her to kick off the afternoon tea—an event she took as seriously as the Super Bowl.

She'd even dressed up for the occasion. Which, for his laid-back girlfriend, meant a white silky blouse tucked into dark jeans and black heels.

Wait a sec. He glanced beneath the table. *Yep.* Just as he suspected. She'd already ditched the shoes. But man, did she have the cutest bare feet. In truth, he found everything about Abby downright adorable, from her frazzled, pink-cheeked perfectionism to the warm, motherly way she fussed over her friends.

He couldn't wait to tell her exactly how he felt about her.

At the thought, his chest swelled, on the verge of bursting. Every fiber in his being burned with excitement, like an electrical current carrying too much voltage. He'd felt the same fire the first time he sat in an F-16, one hand on the side stick, ready for his whole world to change.

The crazy part? Marrying Abby would be a million times more momentous. He just needed her to say yes.

The sugar bowl, resting on the platter, hidden among the scones, suddenly felt heavier than a cargo plane. *Whatever you do, don't look down and draw unnecessary attention.* He shifted the platter in his arms, waiting for Abby to get the party started.

"Everything looks lovely, dear." Verna Hoffstetter beamed from behind a tiered tray of something Abby called petits fours—code for absurdly tiny cakes.

"Thank you." Abby leaned over her friend Sage—who'd seemed distracted since she arrived—to light a tapered candle. "Is it like you remember?"

"My heavens, yes. Very authentic." Verna nodded, and her strange hat nearly toppled off her short tangerine-colored hair. At least, he thought it was a hat. She called it a *fascinator*. Fitting, since it fascinated the heck out of him. The weird netting material had a fake bird sitting on top of it.

"I feel like I'm back in London with my Harold." Verna placed a hand to her heart, her features soft and blissful. He'd never met Verna's late husband, but from the stories Verna told, he would've liked the guy. And he hoped he and Abby would have a similarly long, happy marriage.

His heartbeat accelerated again. If he didn't propose soon, he might keel over from high blood pressure.

"Oh, I'm so glad to hear that!" Abby breathed. "I want everything to be perfect for Sadie and Lucy, and I couldn't have done this trial run without you. Without all of you." She lightly dabbed the corner of her eye with her fingertip, instructing her tears to stay put as her gaze swept their smiling faces.

Besides Verna, Max, and Sage, the partygoers included Abby's best friend, Nadia Chopra, and the Belles—a group of spunky older women who got together under the guise of a book club and philanthropy. Although Logan suspected it had more to do with the snacks and socializing.

"You know we're happy to be guinea pigs anytime food is involved. Right, Max?" Nadia gave Max a gentle nudge with her elbow.

Max grinned, ogling a plate of chocolate eclairs topped with thick, creamy ganache. "Especially dessert."

"Exactly," Nadia agreed. "Now, do we get to eat sometime this century? Or are you going to grab a ruler and start measuring the overhang of the tablecloth?" she teased.

Logan snorted. He liked Nadia. More than he'd expected when they met last Christmas. On first impression, he'd pegged her for a girly-girl who cared too much about brand names and appearances. But he'd quickly upgraded his opinion. Nadia was solid. A fierce, loyal wingman. Or wing*woman*. She'd be a worthy maid of honor to Abby. *If* he ever got the chance to propose.

"Oh!" Abby's eyes widened as she surveyed the lace table-cloth. "I didn't even think about that. Should I?"

"Honey"—Janet Hill flounced her salon-blond curls with an impatient flick of her hand—"while I consider myself to be eighty years *young*, I'd like to live long enough to enjoy this tea while it's still warm."

Abby laughed. "I guess I have gotten a little carried away, haven't I?"

For the first time since he'd paused in the doorway, Abby noticed Logan standing there, holding the scones. Her entire face brightened, and the second their eyes locked, his breath stalled in his throat.

Buckle your seat belts, ladies and gents. We're cleared for takeoff.

"Logan, would you mind setting the scones here, please?" Abby gestured to the only vacant spot on the table.

As if on autopilot, he moved toward her, his pulse thud-ding so loudly he was positive even Verna could hear it from across the room.

He set the platter beside the Spode tea set—the one he'd convinced Abby to use, despite the mismatched sugar bowl.

"Thank you. Now, if you'll take your seat, we're ready to begin." She waved to the empty chair by her side, but Logan didn't budge.

His mouth felt dry and watery at the same time. He swal-lowed clumsily.

"Logan?" Abby cocked her head. "Are you feeling okay?"

Nope, he thought. *Not even a little bit. I'm exhilarated, nervous, excited, fired-up, and pumped so full of adrenaline and eagerness, I might pass out.*

Instead of the lengthy confession, he said, "Yeah. But

there's something I want to give you first." He shifted a few of the scones and lifted the sugar bowl from the platter.

Abby gasped. "How did you—" Her gaze darted to meet his, and he grinned.

"I know a guy."

"I—I can't believe you did this." Her hand flew to her chest, as if she needed to catch her breath. "Of all the crazy, thoughtful, sweet, utterly insane things to do." She laughed, half in disbelief, half in delight. "You outbid me for my sugar bowl!"

"Guilty as charged. Why don't you check out... the, uh, craftsmanship." He stumbled over his words like a tongue-tied teenager asking a girl to prom. *Yeesh.* He must've rehearsed what to say a hundred times, but his mind went blank. As long as he didn't choke on the actual proposal.

He caught the glimmer of Nadia's cell phone camera light as she pressed Record, and his pulse spiked again.

Focus. He fixed his gaze on Abby. Her gorgeous hazel eyes held a questioning glint. And was it his imagination or did her fingers tremble slightly as she reached for the lid?

No one dared breathe as she slowly lifted the lid from the bowl, moving it a millimeter at a time. Another inch and she'd glimpse the diamond ring nestled inside. Another inch and he'd drop to one knee.

"Excuse me," an unfamiliar voice cut through the stillness.

Startled, Abby dropped the lid, and it clattered back onto its base.

Logan's euphoria fizzled into an internal groan of frustration. Seriously? Someone had to interrupt them right *now*?

The unexpected visitor was a woman roughly his own

age, early thirties, give or take a few years. And something about her stance—guarded yet determined, like a soldier at the ready—sent warning bells blaring. A young boy about four or five clung to her hand. "I'm sorry to interrupt," she said without sounding apologetic in the slightest. "But no one answered the door, and I really need to speak to Abigail Preston."

"I'm Abby. How can I help you? Would you like to book a room at the inn?"

"Not exactly." The woman's jaw flexed, and while she aimed her gaze in Abby's direction, she didn't meet her eye—another red flag. He instinctively took a step toward Abby.

"I'd like more than a room," the woman told her. "I'd like half the inn."

"I'm afraid I don't understand." Abby tried to sound calm, but Logan heard the quiver in her voice.

He closed the gap between them, standing by her side for support.

Whatever this woman had to say, it wouldn't be good.

Her gaze darted around the room, confidence wavering. She clearly hadn't expected an audience. Hesitation flickered in her eyes, but her countenance quickly hardened. Her chin rose an inch, and she shifted her stance, sidestepping in front of the boy as if to shield him from her next move.

"Half of this inn belongs to my son, Tyler." For the first time since she'd entered the room, she met Abby's gaze, but Logan couldn't read the woman's muddied expression. Anger? Shame? Sadness? They all blended together. "His father is your late husband. Donnie."

The declaration exploded like a bomb no one saw

coming. Abby took the full brunt of the blast, collapsing against him.

Every muscle in his body tensed as he wrapped his arms around her, his mind struggling to regroup in the fallout.

Today was supposed to change their lives forever.

But not like this.

Chapter 6

ABBY

ABBY SWAYED. Shapes and colors melded together. All sounds, save for her own heartbeat, stilled, muffled by the shock. She barely registered the ground beneath her feet as Logan led her and the other woman into the next room.

The other woman and her *son*.

In the bright light streaming through the sitting room window, she finally focused on the boy's face. Her heart lurched so forcefully, it set her off-balance.

Logan gripped her hand even tighter. "Are you okay?" he whispered.

Her eyes burned. Pressure pushed against her temples, vicious and throbbing. She shook her head, unable to speak.

The boy looked so much like Donnie. The same blond hair the color of lemon pound cake. The same warm brown eyes. Not chocolate brown. Softer, like toasted pecans. He even shared Donnie's thick, dark eyebrows and long lashes.

On appearance alone, he could be Donnie's son. But that was impossible.

Releasing her hand, Logan closed the door to the dining

room. The latch clicked into place, echoing in the thick silence. Except for Logan, all the people she loved most in the world sat behind that wall, waiting. What must they think? What did Logan think? Mortification mixed with confusion, making her sick to her stomach. She tried to make sense of the woman's claim, but she couldn't.

She had to be lying. There wasn't any other explanation.

Standing tall by her side, Logan leveled a cold glare on their uninvited guest. "You've got a lot of nerve—" His gaze fell to the small boy, and he stopped himself.

"Hey, Ty." The woman placed a gentle hand on her son's shoulder. "Why don't you sit over here for a second." She settled him on the couch with a tablet and headphones.

As Abby watched the interaction, a sharp pain twisted in her chest. Was he old enough to understand what was happening? Could he feel the tension in the room? She tried to keep her emotions in check and her demeanor calm for his sake, while internally, her world spiraled out of control.

Once her son was happily focused on cartoons, the woman turned back to face them. "Let's start over. I'm Piper. Piper Sloane. I met Donnie almost six years ago, when I lived in Blessings Bay."

Abby forced herself to look at the woman—*really* look at her—for the first time.

She was admittedly beautiful, in an understated way. Her long blond hair hung in a loose braid down her back. Dark roots poked through, as if she'd missed a few trips to the salon. Shadows sagged beneath her striking green eyes, which she'd tried to hide with carefully applied concealer. But it was the sadness that struck Abby most—deep and piercing. So palpable, she had to look away.

"How did you two meet?" Logan's gruff tone held more than a hint of skepticism.

"I tended bar at the Sawmill. Donnie came in for a drink. We got to talking."

"Donnie didn't drink." Abby finally found her voice, grateful for another crack in the woman's story.

"I know. He told me he usually avoided alcohol because he liked to be in control at all times. But that night, something was different. He said—" Piper hesitated, and the glint of uncertainty in her eyes sent a shiver down Abby's spine. What was she afraid to say?

Piper angled her body toward Logan, as if she wanted to pretend Abby didn't exist. "He said he planned to propose to his girlfriend, but he was having second thoughts."

Abby flinched as if she'd been slapped. "That's not true." Panic fluttered in her chest like a moth trapped in a glass jar heating in the sun. They'd dated for three years before Donnie proposed. Three incredible years, when she'd fallen for him more wholly and deeply every day. When he finally proposed, she hadn't felt a single twinge of doubt. She thought he'd shared her certainty. Was it possible he'd had a fling with this woman before promising to be faithful until death do us part?

"Of course it isn't." Logan narrowed his gaze on Piper, his blue eyes darkening. "I've known Donnie since basic training. He was crazy about Abby. To the point he earned the call sign Romeo, because he couldn't stop gushing about his girlfriend. I've never seen a guy more in love. So, whatever you're selling, I'm not buying."

"Believe me or not, it's the truth. Donnie came to town because his aunt died and left him a house in her will. *This* house. He said the second he saw it, he knew his girlfriend would jump at the chance to live here, but that he'd hate being stuck in a small town. That led him down a rabbit hole, and he realized they wanted different things in life." She glanced over her shoulder at her son before adding softly, "Like kids. He knew his girlfriend wanted a whole football team, and he wasn't sure he wanted any."

As Abby listened, a wave of nausea crashed into her, again and again, making it difficult to stand. How did this woman know all this? Was it possible—? *No. It couldn't be.* Hot tears pooled in her eyes, and she blinked up at the ceiling, willing them away.

"I'd recently been dumped by someone for the same reason," Piper admitted, still speaking to Logan as if Abby wasn't there. "So, when my shift ended, I stayed. We drank. We commiserated. And drank some more. Too much." She glanced at her son again, her features a tangled, tortured mix of love and regret. "It was just one time, but..." She let her voice trail away, and bile rose in Abby's throat.

Stop. Please, stop. She wanted to scream. To plug her ears. To run away. She couldn't bear another word. But she couldn't move. Her heart ached with the same soul-crushing intensity as the day Donnie died, pinning her in place.

"That's enough," Logan growled. He took her hand in a tight, protective grasp.

Abby resisted the urge to bury her face in his shoulder, to block out the ugliness of Piper's words.

"You've clearly done your research," Logan told Piper with poorly disguised disdain. "But not well enough. Your whole scam is bogus and blown to smithereens by one crucial detail. Donnie was physically incapable of having kids."

Abby stole a glance at Piper, expecting her to waver at the news, but the cold statue didn't even blink.

"My thirty-six hours of labor say otherwise."

Abby's gaze fell on the little boy absentmindedly kicking his heels against the couch, engrossed in some silly cartoon, oblivious to the world around him.

He looked so sweet. So innocent. So much like Donnie.

But his existence required two improbabilities.

One, that Donnie betrayed her trust and did the unthinkable. And two, that even though the doctors told them conception would be a one in a million miracle, a single night with this woman resulted in a child. A perfect, beautiful child.

The thought roused another wave of nausea.

"If you don't believe me," Piper challenged, "order a paternity test."

"And how do you suggest we do that?" Logan countered. "Donnie died over a year ago."

"The Air Force will have his DNA records. A laboratory can match them to Tyler in a matter of days if you pay to have the test expedited. We'll wait here until you get the results."

"Here?" Logan repeated, incredulous. "As in, *this inn*?"

At the mere suggestion, Abby's stomach clenched with dread. She gripped Logan's hand tighter.

"Why not? Half of this place belongs to Tyler."

"You're joking." Logan scowled.

"Look." Piper straightened, a few inches shy of standing eye to eye with Logan. "I'm not going anywhere until my son gets the inheritance he deserves. Yes, I should have come forward sooner. But there's no statute of limitations on paternity. And there's nowhere else to stay in Blessings Bay. What do you expect us to do?"

"*Look*," Logan echoed, struggling to keep his cool. "That's not my problem. My first priority is Abby, and I'm not going to let the woman who—"

"They can stay." Abby heard the words escape before her brain had time to process them. Her pulse quickened and sweat slicked her palms, but she couldn't take her eyes off the boy. The boy who looked like Donnie.

"Abby," Logan murmured, his gaze clouded with concern, "you don't have to do this. They can—"

"It's okay." Her voice sounded strange to her own ears— hollow and unfeeling. Resigned. As if she were witnessing a life-ending asteroid, barreling toward Earth, unable to stop it. "We'll expedite the test results, and get it over with as quickly as possible."

"Are you sure?" Logan pressed.

She nodded. But deep in her gut, she wasn't sure about anything anymore.

And that's what scared her the most.

Chapter 7

SAGE

SAGE SLID her bare hands into the wriggling mass of honeybees. The vibration hummed up her arms, and the hundred or so spindly legs tickled her skin. She cupped a handful of little black and yellow bodies, oblivious to the thunderous *buzz, buzz, buzz* filling her ears.

With slow, practiced movements, she shook them into the brood box, but her mind wasn't on the relocation of the rogue swarm. Her tumultuous thoughts careened between boarding the *Marvelous Mira* bright and early tomorrow morning with the man who broke her heart and the upsetting scene that unfolded in Abby's dining room mere hours ago.

She couldn't shake the shell-shocked look on her friend's face when the uninvited guest interrupted their afternoon tea with the ugliest of accusations.

His father is your late husband. Donnie.

As casual as could be, the woman had drawn a damning connection between her son and Abby's late husband. They'd all heard her, clear as a rooster's crow. And yet, no one wanted to believe the allegation. No one wanted to acknowledge what Sage knew all too well—affairs happened. Every second of every day, someone betrayed someone else in the worst possible way. And often, that *someone* was the last person you'd expect.

"Try again. You missed the queen," Grandma Shirley instructed, snapping Sage from her thoughts.

Sure enough, the honeybees had returned to the small sapling where the other worker bees—and their queen—remained huddled together in a pulsating throng.

"Sorry, Gran. I can't seem to focus."

Gran's features softened, and she sat back on her heels, her long bohemian dress splayed around her like a tree skirt. "Abby?"

Sage nodded, the searing sting of compassion pricking her eyes.

For a moment, they knelt in silence, framed by fragrant lavender shrubs, hollyhocks, and foxglove. How many tears had been shed in this very garden? How many heart-rending sobs had been muffled by the border of towering redwoods and sugar pines? How many hurting women had bared their souls to the steadfast honeybees?

"Do you think it's true?" Sage whispered. Her question needed no further explanation. As a member of the Belles, Gran had been present for the shocking ordeal. And like Sage, she'd sat quietly while everyone vehemently refuted the woman's claim. And when Abby explained that the woman and her son would be staying in Blessings Bay—at the inn—until they received the results of a paternity test, they'd remained silent while everyone else offered assurances.

Assurances they couldn't possibly give with any real certainty.

Sage had merely hugged Abby with all her strength and promised to be there for her, no matter what. What else could she do?

"It's possible," Gran admitted gravely. "But if it is, she'll get through it. Abby is strong. And she has us. And there's always room for her here, if she needs it." Gran swept her hand in a broad circle, encompassing the expansive garden, honey-yellow farmhouse, and luxury yurts dotting the verdant forty-acre property overlooking the Pacific Ocean.

Over thirty years ago, Gran opened the Honeybee Retreat as a place for wounded women to heal their broken hearts while immersing themselves in the tranquility of nature. At first, she provided rustic accommodations and minimal amenities. But when Sage's mother took over the operational side of the business—moving them into the farmhouse with Gran right before Sage's sixth birthday—Gran had expanded. She now offered daily yoga, botanical tours, gardening, beekeeping, beachcombing, and home-steading activities. She even held a weekly Bible study, for those who wanted to attend.

Sage loved growing up among the flowers and honeybees. And she enjoyed meeting all the women who stayed at the retreat. Plus, the life lessons—particularly the ones pertaining to men—had been invaluable.

"I hope for Abby's sake, it's all a lie. Or a misunderstand-ing." Sage watched the cluster of bees wrapped around the thin tree trunk, moving as one entity. Almost all of them female. *Oh, the wisdom of bees.*

"Me, too, sweetheart." Gran reached into the center of

the swarm as if picking a ripened peach. The peaceful pollinators encased her hand like a gilded glove, settling into the
brood box without protest. On her first try, Gran had relocated the queen, and the other bees followed.

Sage smiled as Gran gently hummed "Come Together"
by the Beatles, serenading their return. Newcomers to the
Honeybee Retreat always marveled at Gran's boldness when
it came to the bees. She didn't believe in protective suits,
gloves, or even in using smoke to sedate her flying insect
friends.

For as long as she could remember, she'd wanted to be
just like Gran. Fearless. Independent. Unflappable. Her
grandmother hadn't wilted or wallowed in grief when her
husband left. She'd taken her bruised heart and made something beautiful. Something important. Something that made
a difference in people's lives.

And what had Sage accomplished in her twenty-nine
years of life? Not much. She still lived at home and bounced
between part-time jobs, selling the occasional piece of jewelry
she'd made from sea glass, aching for something more mean-
ingful. And until recently, she'd been too afraid to fight for
the one thing she wanted most.

Both Gran and her mother supported her dream to open
a bookstore. Even her bizarre plan to do so on a sailboat. But
when it came to Mackensie's odd proposition—and her decision to live on board said sailboat with Flynn—they each had
their reservations.

"Did you forget something?" Her mother floated into
the garden with all the grace of a forest nymph. At sixty-nine,
Dawn Harper could pass for a much younger woman thanks
to regular yoga, Pilates, and what she called "therapeutic

gardening," an activity Sage learned really referred to aggressive weeding as a form of stress management.

Her mother's midlength flaxen curls grazed her bare shoulders, and the early evening sunlight gave her tanned skin a golden glow. Not for the first time, Sage marveled at how her father could leave someone so stunning and youthful. Particularly for such a tired cliché like his twentysomething secretary.

"What did I forget?" Sage stood and brushed the dirt from her knees.

"I saw all your bags for tomorrow morning stacked by the front door and thought you might want to bring this along." Her mother held out a worn book missing its binding. "You know, to remind you why you're doing all this."

A flood of emotion filled Sage's chest as she read the faded title page. *The Curious Quest of Quinley Culpepper.*

"You must have read that book a hundred times," Gran said, peering over her shoulder.

"More like a thousand." Dawn laughed. "There were many nights I had to pry it out of her hands after she'd fallen asleep."

Sage smiled even as burgeoning tears marred her vision. The adventurous tale about a plucky preteen traveling the world in search of her missing father had been a lifeline during the years after her dad left. It had solidified her love of books and the belief that stories could help heal a broken heart. "Thank you."

"You're sure you want to do this, honeybee?" Her mother brushed a wayward curl away from her face, like she'd done so many times when Sage was a child. "You know Gran and I can help you get a boat some other way."

"I know." Sage pretended to agree, although she knew they couldn't afford it. Every cent went back into the retreat. "I think this is something I need to do on my own. And I'll be fine. Honestly. What happened with Flynn was a long time ago."

Her muscles immediately tensed at the image of Flynn standing near the back of the auction house, aloof and formidable. He looked so different, so unlike himself. The Flynn she knew didn't wear austere suits and leather loafers. He wore linen shirts and deck shoes. His hair wasn't impeccably cut and combed. It was casual and windblown. But his eyes—his eyes had changed the most. Where was the sparkle? The hint of laughter? They'd grown cold. And despite what happened between them, sadness spread over her, sinking into her bones.

Why had Flynn come back to Blessings Bay? And what did he want with Mackensie's sailboat? The Cahills owned dozens of boats, all in better condition than the *Marvelous Mira*.

The Cahills—aka Blessings Bay royalty. They'd never liked her, despite how desperately she'd yearned for their approval. What did they think about their precious son spending three days alone with his socially unsuitable high school sweetheart?

She had a feeling they wouldn't be thrilled with the prospect.

For once, they all had something in common.

FLYNN

"Absolutely not." Randolph Cahill increased the incline on his high-tech treadmill, finally putting his pricey Moncler warm-up suit to work. "I forbid it."

"You forbid it?" Flynn echoed above the techno music his dad swore had been scientifically proven to improve athletic performance.

"What your father means," his mother huffed from the elliptical beside him, "is that living aboard a sailboat for three days with *you know who* isn't a good idea. For multiple reasons."

Flynn loosened his tie, both from frustration and because his parents kept their home gym at a temperature meant to encourage spontaneous sweating. For a couple in their early seventies, their fitness routine rivaled health nuts half their age. His parents wanted to live forever *and* look good doing it. "Is this about the sailboat or about Sage?"

His parents had never approved of Sage. Not from the time he, Sage, and Kevin had become inseparable friends at six years old. And definitely not when he and Sage started dating in high school. They claimed incompatible life philosophies. The Cahills valued wealth, influence, and industrialism. Whereas Shirley, Dawn, and Sage lived on what his parents called a "hippie commune" and sold raw honey at the farmers market with zero aspirations to turn their venture into a Fortune 500 company.

"Don't make this personal," his father grunted, increasing his speed from power walking to a brisk jog. "This is about business. As the new vice president of Cahill Enterprises, you can't play *houseboat* for three days. I don't care who it's with."

Flynn refrained from reminding his father that he wasn't vice president yet. His parents planned to make the big announcement during the Blessings Gala at the end of the week—the whole reason they'd dragged him back home.

They hosted the extravagant event at their clifftop estate every year to raise funds for whichever charity made them look the best. Although outwardly altruistic, Flynn suspected the fancy shindig served to solidify their alpha status. Despite his mother's well-rehearsed platitudes—*We could've left Blessings Bay the moment your father made his first million. But we chose to stay because we love this town. It's our home. Blah, blah, blah*—he knew the score. His parents enjoyed being at the top. It wasn't merely an aesthetic choice that they had the "Cahill compound" built on the highest headland overlooking the entire town.

"I don't have a choice." Flynn helped himself to a glass of ice-cold cucumber water from the crystal dispenser. "Edwin Mackensie laid out the terms. Tomorrow morning, I'll be on board the *Marvelous Mira* looking for his late wife's diary.

You may find this hard to believe, Dad, but he doesn't care about the money."

"Everyone cares about money," his father scoffed. "You simply didn't offer him enough."

Flynn chugged the water, drowning his retort. Of course his father would find a way to make the situation his fault. Never mind that Old Man Mackensie was cuckoo for Cocoa Puffs.

"Sweetheart." His mother softened her tone—a tactic that used to work on him. "We have dozens of boats. You can have any one you want. Take your pick."

"But I don't want just *any* boat. This is the one Kevin wanted."

His mother's step faltered at the mention of his brother's name, and she white-knuckled the handlebars. "It was a trivial childhood dream." She increased the intensity and quickened her stride, as if she could outrun Kevin's memory.

Resentment rose in his chest, crashing against his rib cage. They treated Kevin's death like a dirty secret. Like a stain they could bleach away with stubborn silence. As if bad things couldn't happen to rich people.

His mother dabbed her wrinkle-free forehead, then slid the towel to her temple, suspiciously close to the corner of her eye.

Flynn squinted. Was that a tear? Before he could be sure, she snapped the towel back and tossed it over the handlebar. "Your brother also wanted a prop from that movie he liked so much." She waved a hand at her husband. "You know, the violent one about the gangsters that I still can't believe you let him watch."

"*The Godfather*," Flynn and his father supplied at the same time.

His dad cleared his throat, but not before Flynn caught the raw edge to his voice. *Keep talking*, Flynn silently urged, eager to continue the conversation, to keep his brother's memory alive for as long as possible.

"Right." She nodded, her head bobbing along with her trim body, although her tight bun didn't budge. "It was a hose. Or a watering can. Or something like that. He went on and on about the prop's symbolism, and how he'd own it one day, but we never expected him to actually *buy* the silly thing, did we?"

Flynn held his tongue. The prop in question was a watering gun, and he'd already bought it three years ago after tracking down the collector and offering him an obscene amount of money. Over the last ten years, he'd checked off nearly every item on Kevin's 30 Before 30 bucket list. The list he'd made the summer before college. The summer he died.

He had two items left. Own the *Marvelous Mira*—the custom sailboat Kevin had idolized from the moment he watched it set sail. And become vice president of Cahill Enterprises.

He'd mailed purchase offers to Mackensie every year, begging to buy the boat. But each year, despite Flynn upping the dollar amount, the man refused. If his parents hadn't insisted on his presence at the gala, he never would've known about the auction, let alone been roped into the bizarre proposition they so vehemently opposed. How's that for irony?

Now, with any luck, by the end of the week, he'd have accomplished both remaining tasks.

He wasn't entirely sure what he expected to happen upon the list's completion. It wouldn't bring his brother back. Or make up for the fact that the wrong brother had died that day.

But maybe, in a small way, he could tell Kev he was sorry. Sorry for things he'd never admitted outside the shadows of his own nightmares.

He owed his brother that much, at least.

"I know you guys don't understand, but this is something I have to do," he told them with renewed resolve. "I'll try to mitigate the interference with work as much as possible. And Mom"—he met her gaze in the wall of mirrors—"you don't have to worry. There's zero chance I'll get back together with Sage."

While the words mollified his mother, they evoked an altogether different emotion in the pit of his stomach.

One he'd be wise to ignore.

Chapter 9

ABBY

ABBY TRIED to steady her trembling fingers as she refilled Piper's coffee, ignoring her erratic pulse.

Deep breath. Don't let her get to you.

She inhaled the earthy steam tendrils curling from the cup, willing her tense muscles to relax.

Miraculously, she filled the mug to the brim without spilling a single drop.

"Thanks," Piper said stiffly, barely glancing up from the newspaper, as if she'd rather be eating breakfast in a rabid lion's den than Abby's dining room.

From the moment Piper and her son sat down to eat that morning, she'd appeared painfully uncomfortable. Abby refrained from reminding the woman she was free to leave anytime she wanted.

"These are really good waffles." Tyler beamed at her from across the dining room table, oblivious to the sticky maple syrup dripping down his chin.

"I'm so glad you like them." Abby smiled. She'd made her special Celebration Waffles—so dubbed thanks to the healthy dose of rainbow sprinkles—especially for Tyler. Piper might be a bane, but her son couldn't be sweeter. How could such a lovely child be the product of such a miserable woman?

"They're my favorite breakfast food," Max told Tyler between bites of crispy bacon. "And her Monte Cristo Casserole."

"What's that?" Tyler asked.

"It's like a ham and cheese sandwich and French toast all mushed together." Tyler looked dubious at his description, so Max added, "It's really good," with an air of confidence.

Hiding another smile, Abby rounded the table to top off their orange juices.

Content to take his word for it, Tyler went back to his waffle. He'd flooded each divot with syrup, then topped them with a strawberry slice, exactly like Max. From the moment the boys met, Tyler had taken to Max, as if he craved the attention of another child. In fact, Max didn't usually dine with the guests, but Tyler had begged for Max to join them. Perhaps against her better judgment, Abby had agreed. To his credit, despite Tyler's tendency to follow him around like an adoring puppy, Max didn't seem to mind.

"I get to help cook sometimes," Max said proudly. "I make really good scrambled eggs, right, Abby?"

"The best." She affectionately ruffled his shaggy brown hair, ignoring the sharp pang of longing that afflicted her heart whenever Max said her name. It was too soon for him to call her Mom. She knew that. It could take years for Max to reach that comfort level. *If* he ever did. She knew these things took time. It was normal. Healthy, even. A truth her brain readily accepted, but her heart couldn't seem to grasp.

Piper shot a quick, curious glance across the table, and Abby realized the woman probably knew as little about her personal life as she knew about hers.

To an outsider, she, Logan, and Max looked like the perfect, uncomplicated family. Logan, the doting husband. Max, the adorable son. Abby, the happy homemaker. They ran a successful business, had a beautiful home, and were surrounded by supportive friends. On the outside, they had it all.

No one knew Abby lay awake most nights, wondering if the boy she'd come to love like a son would one day be ripped from her arms. Or if she had a future with the man who'd stolen her heart while he'd gently mended the broken pieces.

She'd thought maybe Logan had been about to propose yesterday. He'd been so keen for her to open the sugar bowl. And if nervous energy could create electricity, he could've powered all of Blessings Bay. In that moment, the joy of anticipation had washed over her, bathing her in pure, unbridled bliss.

Then Piper arrived, blowing up her past *and* her present.

Instead of celebrating an engagement, she'd spent the morning making phone calls to DNA laboratories and military medical offices, fighting tears as she explained the need for a paternity test. Mortification, grief, and uncertainty had become her constant companions, taking turns as the predominant emotion. She'd barely slept or eaten, concentrating solely on making it through this nightmare, back to the way things used to be before Piper ruined everything.

If Logan *had* been about to propose, he would try again, wouldn't he?

She pulled a dishrag from the front pocket of her apron

and wiped the dribble of syrup oozing down the crystal dispenser. Would she even want Logan to propose right now, in the midst of this mess?

She cast a sideways glance at Piper, bent over the *Blessings Bay Gazette*, sipping coffee in between nibbles of buttered toast. A tight coil of resentment wound around Abby's heart. Did Piper have any idea what she'd done? How many lives she'd impacted? Did she even care?

Piper's phone buzzed on the table. She glanced at the screen, and her face immediately paled. "I'll be right back." She snatched her cell and abandoned her breakfast, rushing from the room with unsettling swiftness.

Abby's mind raced with possibilities. Could someone close to Piper be in the hospital and the doctor called with an update? Or maybe Piper herself was unwell and waiting on test results? At the thought, unwanted compassion overshadowed her resentment.

Abby pushed all sympathy-inducing hypothetical scenarios out of her mind. She did *not* want to feel sorry for this woman.

She sat with the boys while they finished breakfast, waiting for Piper to return. What was taking her so long?

"Can I go to school with Max today?" Tyler asked.

"I don't think so, sweetheart," Abby said, her gaze still glued on the door. "You're not enrolled. And you're in different grades, so you wouldn't be in the same class, anyway."

"I'm in kindergarten. But Mom says I get to have summer break early. She says we're going on an ad-ven-ture." He puffed up his chest, proud of himself for enunciating such a big word.

"How fun. And what do you think of your adventure so far?"

"It's okay." Tyler shrugged, then grinned at Max. "I like this part the best."

Abby smiled for Tyler's benefit, not wanting him to feel unwelcome, despite the pain their presence had caused.

She glanced at the clock. Max would need to leave for school soon. Where was Piper? Abby stood and strode toward the door. Cracking it open, she poked her head into the hallway.

Piper hovered against the wall, hunched over her phone. "I need more time." Her hushed tone made Abby's pulse spike. What was she talking about?

"Give me a few more days. Please." Piper's plea cracked with desperation, and an icy chill slipped down Abby's spine. Why did she need more time? What was going on?

Max's and Tyler's gleeful chatter carried through the open door, and Piper turned, eyes wide.

Abby whipped backward and yanked the handle.

The door swung shut.

Had Piper seen her?

Her heart raced.

She hadn't intended to eavesdrop. But from Piper's panicked expression, she'd overheard something she shouldn't have.

Only, she had no idea what the cryptic conversation meant.

Chapter 10

LOGAN

Logan stuffed the leftover lingonberry muffins into a large Tupperware, keeping an eye on Abby as she zigzagged around the kitchen, cleaning up after breakfast. She'd insisted on serving Piper and Tyler herself, no matter how many times he'd bemoaned the idea. She shouldn't have to serve the woman claiming to be her husband's one-night stand. But Abby wouldn't relent and shooed him out of the house to do the week's grocery shopping.

Somehow, Abby seemed to be holding it together, despite the rickety roller coaster Piper had strapped them all into the moment she arrived. Thankfully, she'd retreated back to her room after breakfast, with Tyler in tow. No more bombs dropped today. Not that she could get any more nuclear than claiming Donnie had a secret love child. I mean, seriously? Donnie cheating on Abby? You couldn't get more implausible. Not to mention the blatant impossibility thanks to the whole shooting-blanks situation.

A fresh surge of anger ripped through him, and his muscles involuntarily tensed.

"Easy, Hulk." Abby's teasing tone broke through his thoughts. "People actually like to eat those."

He looked down, realizing he'd smashed one of the muffins in his tightly wound fist. "Shoot. Sorry, Abs. What a mess." He grabbed a dish towel and swept the crumbs into a pile.

"It's fine. I can use the muffins in a blueberry crumble later. But if you need a stress ball, may I suggest one of these instead?" She offered him a Meyer lemon. "I plan to make some lemonade later this afternoon, and you can save me some time."

Abby flashed a genuine smile for the first time that morning. Her entire face brightened like the sun rising above the clouds, and Logan couldn't help himself. He tossed the dish towel on the counter and pulled her into his arms, sealing her lips with his as if a single kiss could rewind time. As if they could return to the moment before Piper arrived. To the moment when he'd planned to ask Abby to marry him.

Piper hadn't just wiped her muddy boots on the past. She'd stomped all over their future, too. At least Abby didn't know about that part yet.

When he finally let Abby come up for air, she gasped, her hazel eyes shining. "What was that for?"

"Because you're amazing. Because, in the midst of this craziness, you can still smile. And you know your smile gets me every time."

She laughed softly, resting snug in his arms. "Well, it helps that you're so indignant on my behalf. It's like you're carrying the burden of outrage for me, so I don't have to."

"Happy to be of service. But seriously, how are you doing? It can't be easy having her here." He'd reminded

Abby a dozen times that she didn't have to let Piper stay at the inn, but she hadn't changed her mind.

"I'm fine." She averted her gaze, a sure sign she wasn't being entirely truthful. To top it off, she wriggled away, resuming her after-breakfast cleanup.

He watched her dump the dirty casserole dish into the sink of soapy water, and his heart wrenched. He hated to see her hurting. Especially here, in her happy place.

He'd lived in this house for years, maintaining the massive historic mansion and sprawling acre of land, but it had never felt like a home before. The sunny, spacious kitchen had merely been a place to prepare his meals. And not even good ones. Although, he had learned to be creative with a can of tuna, if he did say so himself.

Since Abby moved in—and he'd relocated to the bungalow in the backyard—the house hadn't just become a warm and inviting home. She'd made it special. And not only for him and Max. For everyone. People came to Blessings on State Street to relax and unwind. To enjoy themselves. Or, as the inn's new tagline described it—thanks to Nadia's genius marketing skills—it was a place where luxury and leisure met hometown hospitality.

Then Piper mucked it all up by dragging her lies and drama through the front door. Now, tension stretched through the walls, putting everyone on edge.

"I know what fine stands for," Logan told her. "Fine means *feelings inside not expressed*." He'd heard the cheesy acronym on a self-help podcast pumped into the waiting room at his doctor's office. Funny how his brain remembered that little ditty, but not his email password.

Abby wailed on the baking dish, flinging soap suds into

the air as she scrubbed. "I can't let Piper know she got to me."

"Why not?"

"Because I don't want her to think she can intimidate me with her lies. I don't want her to think for one second that I believe her." Abby continued to scour with so much fervor, water sloshed onto the counter and soaked the front of her apron.

"And you don't, right?" Logan joined her at the sink, putting himself in the splash zone. "You don't believe her, do you?"

"Of course not." The deep farmhouse sink resembled a wave pool, and Logan placed a hand on her arm, calming the motion.

"Abs," he murmured, gently removing the sponge from her death grip. "It's okay to not be okay. Even if you know she's lying."

She looked up and met his gaze, tears welling in her eyes. "But what if she isn't? There's a slim chance she could be telling the truth." Her pained, whispered words punched him in the stomach. He'd give anything to erase her doubt.

"She's not."

"How do you know?"

"Because if Donnie loved you even half as much as I do, the thought of being with another woman would make his skin crawl." He shivered to drive home his point. "See? Just talking about it is giving me the heebie-jeebies."

"Okay, you made your point." She cracked a small smile and added, "Thanks."

Logan grinned, happy she looked reassured. "Besides, even if we ignore reality for a second and pretend that

Donnie really is Tyler's father, Piper wouldn't have waited this long to show up. She would've asked Donnie for child support years ago."

"That's true. There is something off about her. Like she's hiding something."

"Yeah. She *is* hiding something—the truth. Seriously, Abs. There are so many holes in her story, it looks like target practice." The pep talk seemed to be working, so he stopped while he was ahead. No reason to mention the tiny, niggling questions still bothering him. Like, what exactly *was* the connection between Piper and Donnie? She knew too much to be a complete stranger. And why had Donnie kept the house a secret from Abby for all those years? Something didn't add up.

"You're right. Thank you. I feel much better." She glanced at the antique clock on the wall. "If you don't leave soon, you'll miss the bus."

"I thought I'd stick around here today. Stress-squeeze some lemons. Maybe squish a few more muffins."

"Nope." Abby shook her head. "As much as I appreciate your superior grip strength, you're not missing your doctor's appointment on my account. Not when they've been going so well."

"But that's exactly why I *can* afford to miss one. Doc gave me a gold star at my last appointment. He says I'm making good progress." Logan hadn't wanted to get his hopes up too high, but after months of working with a specialist to reduce his sporadic muscle spasms—a fun little present from the spinal injury that got him kicked out of the Air Force—he'd finally seen improvement.

"You're proving my point. You shouldn't interrupt your

progress." Abby's tone said, *Don't even try to argue with me, mister.* "Besides, I have it all under control. I spoke to a DNA testing laboratory this morning. They're sending a swab kit for Tyler. And once the Air Force releases Donnie's DNA records, they can have the results in forty-eight hours. With any luck, this whole ordeal will be over in a few days."

In awe, he leaned against the counter, forgetting about the deluge of dishwater. It dampened the back of his T-shirt, but he didn't care. "You're incredible. You know that, right?"

"So I've been told."

"And I'm going to keep telling you." He almost added *for the rest of our lives* but held off. He'd get a proposal do-over someday, but not today. Soon, he hoped. He wasn't sure how much longer he could wait. There were times he literally ached to marry her, to finally merge every aspect of their lives —of *themselves*—together. His scrawny one-bedroom bungalow had started to feel a little too lonely these days.

After another kiss goodbye, he headed outside to catch the bus at the end of Main Street. Not his favorite mode of transportation, but until he got the muscle spasms under control, he refused to drive and put others at risk. He'd use the downtime to Google Piper Sloane on his phone. Maybe he'd get lucky and find something useful.

As he crossed the front lawn, he spotted Verna Hoffstetter emerging from her light-purple Queen Anne Victorian across the street. The color reminded him of grape-flavored saltwater taffy. Mr. Bingley—affectionately dubbed Bing—waddled a few steps behind. The chubby English bulldog could stand to lose a few pounds, not that he'd tell Verna. If she put him on a diet, Bing would never forgive him.

"Hey, Verna." He stopped at the curb to greet her, briefly stooping to scratch Bing behind the ears.

"How's our girl?" Verna asked in lieu of hello.

"Tough as titanium," he told her. "And a far better person than I am. She's treating Piper as if she's any other guest. I would've given her a first-class ticket to Get Outta Town."

Okay, so maybe he wouldn't have been quite that heartless. Sure, he had zero respect for Piper, but she had a five-year-old son. Tyler didn't ask for this. He seemed like a sweet kid. His mom might be an opportunist charlatan, but Tyler wasn't. In some ways, he was a victim, too. What kind of mother involved her own son in such an underhanded scheme? He'd keep an eye on them. If he suspected the kid was in any harm, he wouldn't hesitate to intervene.

"Our Abby is kindhearted," Verna cut into his thoughts. "But she's no pushover. There's a reason she let that woman stay."

"You're probably right. I jumped straight into fix-it mode without really considering Abby's motivation," he admitted. But his wife-to-be wasn't a damsel in distress. She was a fighter. And often, a whole lot smarter than him.

"Whatever her plan is," Verna said, "we'll be with her every step of the way." Her eyes sparkled with a mischievous glint. "I called the Belles. We suddenly needed to reschedule our weekly book club meeting to today, and we thought Piper might like to join us."

Logan grinned at the visual of Piper being grilled by five feisty octogenarians. "I'll look forward to the debriefing."

"We'll happily share our intel. There's something off

about that woman. Like she's hiding more than a secret affair."

"I think you're right, Verna. And apparently, so does Bing."

The pudgy-faced pup sniffed the back tire of Piper's black four-door Jeep parked along the curb.

"What is it, bud? What d'ya smell?" Logan stepped closer and peered into the faintly tinted windows. The entire back seat disappeared beneath Tyler's car seat, bulging duffel bags, dirty clothes, blankets, toys, stuffed animals, boxes of snack food, and two cases of bottled water. His heart lurched. Were they living in their car?

"That's odd," Verna said, snooping over his shoulder.

"You're telling me. Either they're fleeing a crime or preparing for the apocalypse," he teased, but the joke fell flat. His stomach turned with worry for Tyler. They *could* be witnessing the aftermath of a long road trip, he supposed. But Piper said they'd traveled seven hours. Was this level of chaos a reasonable result?

"Do you think this woman and her son are in some kind of trouble?" Verna asked, her hushed tone mirroring his concern.

"I don't know," he admitted. "But I intend to find out."

Chapter 11

ABBY

ABBY ARRANGED small jars filled with colorful sprinkles on the antique table formerly reserved for fresh floral arrangements and travel brochures while Tyler wiggled in his seat, drooling over the tray of plain sugar cookies.

From this vantage point, she had a clear view of the Belles on the other side of the sitting room.

Each woman sat in her usual spot. Gail Lewis and Janet Hill occupied the twin wingbacks—Gail with her impeccable posture and Janet lounging with her legs crossed. Faye Thompson, in her brocade skirt and vest combo, blended into the vintage Rococo chair. Verna shared the sofa with Sage's grandmother, Shirley Milton, who, from the pinched expression on Verna's face, wore a little too much patchouli today.

While they each held a copy of *The Secret Book of Flora Lea*, they weren't focused on the open pages. Their collective gaze illuminated the love seat like an interrogation lamp. Piper sat in the middle, sinking into the plump cushions as if she hoped to disappear inside.

Abby almost felt sorry for the woman. The Belles had roped her into their book club, resolutely ignoring her many attempts to decline. When Piper mentioned she hadn't read the book, Janet admitted that she hadn't, either. "I come for the good food and the gossip," she'd said. "You'll fit right in."

Piper used Tyler as her next excuse, but Verna gave a dismissive wave of her hand. "Oh, Abby can look out for him," she'd offered. "She's always coming up with fun activities for Max. She can keep him busy while we ladies chat."

Piper looked mortified by the prospect, but Verna and the Belles wouldn't take no for an answer. Hence, the impromptu sugar cookie decorating.

Abby situated six cookies on a sheet of parchment paper —three flower cutouts and three ladybugs. She'd also assembled a plethora of supplies, including her best piping nozzles. Probably overkill for a five-year-old, but she wanted him to have options.

"Does this have Red 40 or Yellow 5?" Tyler squinted at the jar of rainbow sprinkles, his chubby little face scrunched with concern.

Abby blinked. How did he know about food dyes? "No, they don't."

"What about those?" He pointed to the pastry bags stuffed with frosting.

"Nope. I never use artificial coloring in my cooking."

"Good. 'Cause my mom doesn't let me eat that stuff. She said it's a 'spiracy between FDR and Big Pharma to make us sick." He lisped when he tried to pronounce *conspiracy*, and Abby bit back a laugh.

"You mean the FDA?"

"Yeah, him. And the other guy. They're bad dudes," Tyler told her with adorable earnestness.

"They sure sound like it." Abby matched his serious tone, hiding her surprise. She hadn't pegged Piper for the kind of mother who worried about food dyes and artificial ingredients. Dragging Tyler halfway across the state in some fraudulent paternity scheme didn't exactly scream *stellar mom material*.

As she set the rest of the cookie-decorating utensils on the parchment paper, she couldn't stop the unwelcome thoughts from invading her mind. What if she and Donnie *had* been able to conceive? Would their child have been anything like Tyler? Would she have been a good mother back then?

A familiar tightness crept up her chest, and she swallowed, shoving her emotions—and all the haunting what-ifs—deep inside where they belonged.

Forcing a smile, she helped Tyler get started on a ladybug, then surreptitiously turned her attention toward the conversation happening across the room.

"So, ladies. What did you think of the book?" Verna asked her cohorts.

"I loved it. Five stars from me." Faye smiled, and her full, round cheeks shifted her glasses slightly higher on the bridge of her nose.

While she didn't doubt Faye's sincerity in this instance, Abby couldn't imagine the kindhearted, cajoling woman rating a book anything less than five stars. Even if she *didn't* love it.

"Would you say it was historically accurate, Gail?" Faye asked.

Gail sipped her tea, pondering the question before announcing in her authoritative, retired-history-teacher tone, "Yes. As far as fiction *can* be accurate, Faye."

Abby braced herself for one of Gail's lectures on how creative liberties needed to be balanced with exhaustive research when Verna interjected.

"What fascinated me," she said, "is the concept of *secrets*. *Secrets* can be quite complicated, can't they?" Verna looked directly at Piper, overenunciating the word *secrets* to a less-than-subtle effect.

"I suppose so." Piper shifted in her seat, carefully balancing her teacup and saucer as she squirmed.

"There's also the theme of storytelling," Verna continued. "And how stories can impact our lives, for better or worse. Isn't that interesting?" Once again, Verna directed her question at Piper.

"Sure. I guess." Piper gulped her tea, looking so uncomfortable, Abby felt a tiny pang of guilt—a pang she quickly squelched.

"*Stories*," Verna said, placing extra emphasis on the word again, "can be quite wonderful, even cathartic, when used for good. But when used for ill will or ill-gotten gains, they can be rather damaging, don't you think?"

Piper reached for an almond raspberry tea cake, avoiding Verna's question altogether this time.

Was it her imagination, or had Piper read between the lines of Verna's literary musings? The Belles might not get as much out of their target as they'd hoped.

As if she'd had the same inkling, Janet snapped the paperback shut and tossed it on the coffee table. "Enough about the book. Tell us about yourself, Piper. Where are you from?" Leaning forward, she flashed her warmest we're-all-friends-here smile.

"Down south."

"South like Los Angeles? San Diego? Or south of the border?" Janet asked in a casual, chatty tone.

"From a small town. You wouldn't have heard of it." Piper reached for another tea cake, and when she wasn't looking, Janet threw up her hands in defeat.

Gail rolled her eyes at how quickly Janet surrendered, and Abby smiled. Gail, strict and regimented, frequently chided Janet for her lack of discipline and follow-through when it came to anything other than her rigorous antiaging routine. "What do you do for work?" Gail asked Piper, taking over as interrogator.

"I—" Piper paused, appearing to weigh her words carefully before adding, "I'm in transition right now."

"Career change?" Gail pressed for more details.

"Yes," Piper said simply, finishing her tea cake.

"And what do you do for fun? I love to crochet," Faye chirped, clearly not understanding the assignment. "Do you enjoy crochet?"

"Not really."

"Do you plan to stay in town long?" Shirley prodded, redirecting the conversation.

Abby's pulse raced, and she tried to read Piper's expression from the corner of her eye, without looking too interested. But she *had* questioned Piper's game plan more than a hundred times since yesterday. Surely, Piper knew the DNA results would come back negative. What would she do then? Why drive all that way for a plan doomed to fail? It didn't make sense.

"For as long as it takes." Piper drained her last sip of tea and set the cup and saucer on the coffee table. Facing the women in turn, she added, "Look. I know you ladies don't like me. And frankly, I don't care. I'm not here to make friends. The only thing you need to know about me is that I'm here for my son. And if any of you are mothers, maybe you can try to understand that." She rose from the love seat, her features firmly set with a level of confidence and conviction that made Abby's blood freeze. "Tyler."

He looked up from the ladybug cookie he was decorating as if his mother's voice were the only sound capable of breaking his concentration. "Yeah?"

"Let's take a walk down to the beach."

"Okay!" He brightened at the suggestion. "Can I bring the cookies?"

"You may bring *one*."

He grinned, and to Abby's surprise, turned back around to tidy up the table, starting with replacing the sprinkle caps. How many five-year-olds voluntarily cleaned up after themselves?

"It's okay," she told him. "I can clean up. You go with your mom." On impulse, she asked Piper, "Would you like to take some sand toys?"

For a moment, Piper stared at her as if she'd sprouted two heads, both of which were unexpectedly nice to her. "No." After a short pause, she added, "Thank you."

Tyler scooped the cookie into his hands and scampered after his mom.

Before the door swung shut, Tyler waved goodbye, his little face smiling wide as if she'd become his new best friend.

Abby waved back, returning his smile as the fragile fissures sinewing through her heart slowly split open.

Was there even the tiniest possibility that Piper wasn't lying after all?

And if so, could she bear to uncover the truth?

Chapter 12

SAGE

SAGE EXHALED a heavy breath as an unexpected truth settled in her heart.

She was going to miss this place.

The warm, velvety rays of sunrise streamed through the large front windows, bathing CeCe's café in soft sepia tones. Sage blinked back tears as the familiar shapes of polished tabletops and plump, cozy armchairs nestled around a smooth stone fireplace blurred before her eyes.

She'd taken the part-time job at CeCe's to pay the bills, but it had become so much more. She'd miss the quiet lull before the doors opened to customers, when baker extraordinaire, CeCe Dupree, filled the entire café with the most mouthwatering aromas, from savory sourdough to sweet beignets. She didn't even mind the 5 a.m. wail of her alarm clock since it meant an hour of one-on-one time with her busy best friend before the first customer bustled through the front door.

"Are you *sure* this is a good idea?" CeCe burst through

the swinging door from the kitchen, her arms laden with a tray of fresh-from-the-oven baguettes.

"No. It's a terrible idea. But I don't really have a choice." She'd just finished regaling CeCe with the details of Edwin Mackensie's proposition, and her friend still couldn't wrap her head around the absurd assignment, although she'd given her the next three days off despite her reservations.

"But you and Flynn. Alone. For three whole days." CeCe shook her head, nearly undoing her disheveled topknot of thick black hair. "That's like putting the Romulans and Klingons on the same starship and not expecting a bloodbath."

Sage laughed. "I don't know what concerns me more. That you're right, or that I finally understand your geeky *Star Trek* references."

"I knew our *Next Generation* marathon would pay off." CeCe grinned and slid a baguette into a crinkling brown paper sleeve. She added the still-steaming bread to the cavernous canvas tote bag bursting with half a dozen other loaves she'd already stuffed inside, amplifying their buttery scent.

"But seriously." CeCe met her gaze across the lacquered cedar countertop, worry reflected in her wire-rimmed glasses. "Doesn't the fact that you'll be stuck on a sailboat together seem sort of morose given your history?"

Sage twisted her finger around the handle of her coffee mug, willing the unwanted memories away. If she concentrated hard enough, she barely even remembered the day Flynn left her standing alone on the dock, desperately clinging to the fractured remnants of her shattered heart. "That was a long time ago. We were kids. He's moved on. I've moved on. It's all in the past."

CeCe raised an eyebrow. "So, I guess we're going to pretend like I believe you?"

"That would be great." Sage shot her friend a wry grin, hoping to lighten the mood.

CeCe rolled her eyes but returned the smile, anyway. "I'll let it slide this time. But when the next three days are over, we're going to overanalyze every single detail until we've talked for so long, we've both lost our voices. Got it?"

"'Make it so.'" Sage saluted, quoting the catchphrase of CeCe's favorite *Star Trek* captain, Jean-Luc Picard.

"I'm not sure you're using that right, but I appreciate the effort." CeCe laughed, loading a pastry box with profiteroles before dusting them with confectioners' sugar. Thanks to her overzealous sifting, the silky white powder plumed from the sieve, speckling her dark skin like freshly fallen snow.

Sage resisted the urge to reach across the counter and brush aside the flecks, capturing the mental image instead. CeCe's bright, unfiltered smile. The apron that read *Made of Pie Crust and Stardust*. The way her onyx eyes always seemed to look right through her, to her heart and soul.

CeCe was the one person who knew all her secrets, dreams, and hidden heartaches. She'd been there for her when Kevin's accidental drowning devastated the entire town. And then when Flynn left Blessings Bay without a single word, least of all a goodbye.

Through it all, CeCe remained ever faithful, ever steady. What would she do without her?

Tears welled in her eyes again. "Maybe I shouldn't go. Maybe opening a bookstore on a sailboat is a bad idea."

"It's a great idea," CeCe assured her. "I'm sorry I filled

your head with second thoughts. Don't worry about Flynn. I'm sure it'll be fine."

"It's not that. Well, not *just* that. But on the off chance this wild scheme doesn't end in total disaster, we won't work together anymore. I'm not sure I'm ready for that much change. I'll miss you too much."

"The change will be a good thing. Besides, we'll still see each other all the time. The marina is only a stone's throw away. Literally. I could throw a rock from my patio and hit your sailboat."

"I guess." Sage tried to smile, but once she opened her bookshop—*if* she opened her bookshop—they'd both be business owners with endless responsibilities. A reality that simultaneously thrilled and intimidated her. Although, it was usually the latter. Especially when her ever-present insecurities whispered familiar phrases like *You're not good enough. What makes you think you can do this? You'll probably fail.*

CeCe finagled the pastry box into the overstuffed bag, then stuck a full pound of coffee on top.

"You realize I'll only be on board the *Marvelous Mira* for three days," Sage reminded her. "And Edwin Mackensie offered to provide all the essentials, even groceries. You don't have to pack half the bakery."

"Except you can't cook. And without coffee, you're crankier than a Cardassian with a neck cramp." CeCe rattled off another *Star Trek* reference as if her extreme level of nerdiness was normal. "Flynn's already incurred your wrath. He won't stand a chance if you're uncaffeinated, too."

"Fair enough," Sage conceded, ignoring the way her stomach clenched at the mention of Flynn's name. "Thanks for giving me the time off, especially on such short notice."

"Of course! If it means you finally get to open your bookstore, I'm on board. Pun intended," CeCe teased. "Besides, I've heard about Edwin Mckensie's eccentric shenanigans, but I've never been this close to one. I kinda want to see how it plays out."

"Glad my misery can provide some entertainment," Sage said with playful sarcasm.

"I mean, all you have to do is throw in a cute dog, and you're basically starring in one of Jayce's movies." CeCe blushed, as she did every time she mentioned their childhood friend turned mega Hollywood star Jayce Hunt. But for once, Sage breezed over CeCe's lifelong unrequited crush, intent on setting the record straight.

"Except, Jayce only stars in romantic comedies. And there is zero chance Flynn and I will be sailing off into the sunset. *Zero*," she added for emphasis.

Thankfully, CeCe had the good sense not to respond. She slid the overflowing tote bag across the countertop. "You'd better hurry. You're supposed to be at the marina in five minutes, and you don't want Flynn to get a head start on finding that diary."

Sage drained the last drop of her lavender honey latte and hopped off the stool. "Wish me luck."

CeCe rounded the front counter and enveloped her in a hug. "Three days will be over before you know it."

Sage sincerely hoped so, but as her sandals slapped against the wooden dock mere minutes later, time seemed to slow with each footstep. Apprehension built in her chest, crowding out her lungs.

Breathe. In and out. In and out.

She concentrated on each breath, matching the rhythm

to the gentle lapping of waves against the pilings. Internally, every impulse screamed for her to turn and run. Outwardly, she raised her chin an inch higher, feigning confidence.

Don't let Flynn see how much he hurt you. Be strong. Be impassive.

The *Marvelous Mira* loomed ahead, moored in the last slip at the end of the dock. The main mast partially obscured the sun, splitting it down the middle, scattering streaks of bronzed light on either side. Her pulse quickened. Even after months beached ashore a small uninhabited island, sun-bleached and weather-beaten, the svelte schooner was easily the prettiest boat at Blessings Marina. And to think, in a few days, she could be hers.

Sage tightened her grip on her duffel bag, careful not to shift the heavy tote slung over one shoulder. Her heart pounded, vibrating with the force of a hundred honeybees humming in unison... until her gaze fell on Flynn, standing beside Herman Chesterfield near the gangway. Their eyes met, and the frantic beating stopped instantly, as if he'd thrown a switch. As if he still had control over her heart, even after all these years.

Each carefully controlled breath evaporated, leaving her light-headed. She reached for a railing for support, but her fingertips met air. She had nothing to hold her steady. Nothing to ease the dizziness. She could only hope Flynn felt equally disoriented.

No such luck.

He smiled when he saw her—actually smiled!—like her presence didn't evoke unbearable dread and discomfort. The nerve! He should be sweating. Or squirming. Anything but smiling.

She glared when she should've glanced away. She didn't need to see how good he looked in his light-blue polo and linen shorts. Or the way his chestnut hair ruffled in the salty breeze. Her fingers had once combed through those windswept strands. They'd traced the tender spot behind his ear, down the curve of his neck, making his toes curl. Sage wet her lips. Her mouth felt dry, as if she'd swallowed buckets of sand, and heat blazed across her skin. Mortified by the intimate memory, she tore her gaze away from Flynn, only to glimpse something equally unnerving.

An adorable golden retriever sat by Flynn's feet, gazing at her with the most beautiful heart-melting brown eyes.

CeCe's words flooded her mind. *Throw in a cute dog, and you're basically starring in one of Jayce's movies.* Sage groaned. Great. Just what she needed.

"You bought a dog?" she blurted before she could stop herself. Dog lover didn't jibe with her image of Flynn as a soulless corporate sellout.

"Technically, I didn't buy him. We sort of found each other five years ago. It's a long story." He turned to Herman. "Hope it's not breaking any rules if Cap tags along. I couldn't leave him with my parents. Their version of pet-sitting is a bowl of water and a flat-screen set on an endless loop of *Animal Planet*."

"I don't anticipate that Mr. Mackensie will mind."

As Flynn scratched the scruff at the pup's neck, Sage suppressed an irrational, inexplicable, utterly irritating sliver of envy.

Five years. He can commit to a dog, but not you.

Ugh. She was jealous. Of a dog. She'd sunk to a new low.

"Shall we get started?" Herman interjected. "I'll need to lay out a few ground rules before I leave you."

Before I leave you. The words echoed inside her head, loud and ominous. She contemplated begging Herman to stay as some sort of buffer. Maybe she could bribe him with a binge session of *The Great British Bake Off*?

"Let me guess," Flynn said. "The boat's rigged with sensors, so Mackensie will know if one of us tries to bolt. Or throws the other person overboard." He caught her eye and flashed a wry grin.

Her traitorous stomach did a somersault. *Cut it out.* Sure, she used to find his playful personality charming. And his easy, fun-loving smile used to make her swoon. *Used to*, past tense. Before she learned the hard way that Flynn Cahill may have charisma, but he didn't have character. A far more important quality.

She frowned, shooting him a look that said, *Can we stay on track, please?*

"Mr. Mackensie is abiding by the honor system," Herman told them. "But he wanted to let you know that he's made sure the head and galley are in working order. And all provisions are to be shared equally."

Relief raced through her. With all her worrying about today, she hadn't even considered the condition of the bathroom and kitchen. Thankfully, Edwin Mackensie had. But why had he gone to so much trouble to fix a boat he planned to sell for next to nothing? He'd just leapfrogged from eccentric to certifiable.

"Any questions before you embark?" Herman glanced between her and Flynn.

"Just one," Flynn said. "How many beds are there?"

"I believe there's only one, sir."

At Herman's far-too-casual confession, Sage's stomach vaulted before plummeting into a free fall. *No way.* This wasn't happening. Under no circumstances would she share a bed with Flynn "Can't Be Counted On" Cahill. She'd sooner sleep topside with a life buoy as a pillow than sleep in the same *room* with him, let alone the same bed.

She couldn't bring herself to look at Flynn. But for a split second, from the corner of her eye, she thought she caught the faintest of smiles. A possibility that didn't upset her as much as it should.

Chapter 13

FLYNN

FLYNN STOOD ROOTED to the dock, his gaze following Herman and Sage as they boarded the *Marvelous Mira*.

Cap shimmied his backside, eager to embark, but waiting patiently for Flynn to get his act together.

Flynn tightened his grip on Cap's leash but still didn't budge.

Come on. One foot in front of the other.

He tried to cajole his body into motion, but his brain kept his feet glued in place, working overtime to sort through his conflicted emotions.

Despite his love for the wide-open water, he hadn't been near a sailboat since his brother's death. Too many painful memories. Besides, forgoing his greatest passion in life while pursuing Kevin's was a fitting consequence for the selfish choice he'd made ten years ago. The day his brother died.

"Are you coming?" Sage called from the starboard deck. "Or are you giving up already?" Her inflection indicated she wouldn't be surprised if he quit.

Even in his current condition, with his body and brain at

odds, she did something to him on a molecular level. Something he couldn't explain. The feeling reminded him of the first time he set sail, when the wind and water came together like art, physics, and magic all rolled into one. His stomach sank while his heart soared, wholly transcendent and intoxicating. He couldn't get enough. And after all these years, she still had the same effect. How was that possible?

He squinted in the sunlight, taking in her ethereal appearance. Her hair shone in the golden light, fluttering gently in the briny sea breeze. The long skirt of her white cotton sundress billowed around her legs like a sail, drawing his focus to her slender ankles—and the braided friendship bracelet she still wore.

He closed his eyes. The moment she'd given him and Kevin their matching bracelets remained imprinted on his mind. Life had been so simple then. The future had been bright and promising, brimming with the call of adventure. And now?

Now, all love and joy and hope for something better lay buried with his brother.

"Are you okay?" Her tone softened slightly, and he realized he'd grimaced, pained by the memory.

"Peachy." He cleared his throat, returning to the present. "Just caught a glare while I admired my new boat." He tossed a teasing grin in her direction, grateful he could hide his pain with humor.

Sage rolled her eyes and turned her back to him.

Patting Cap's head, he murmured, "Ready, boy?"

Cap nudged his palm for moral support, and Flynn straightened.

It's now or never.

Letting Cap lead, he crossed the gangway, his heart thudding inside his chest with each step.

Three days. He could keep it together for that long, couldn't he?

As Herman gave his little spiel, reiterating the rules and Mackensie's expectations—find the diary, blah, blah, blah—Flynn let his gaze wander. Even after weeks lost at sea, the *Marvelous Mira* was a bona fide babe. Easily the classiest boat he'd ever seen, and his parents had dozens scattered along both coastlines.

Her white paint needed a fresh coat, and the rigging looked worn. He wouldn't know about the sails until he unfurled them, but he had a hunch they'd seen better days. All in all, there was a good chance the *Marvelous Mira* wasn't even seaworthy. But what did it matter? It wasn't like he planned to set sail. It would be good enough to simply own her.

Herman continued their tour below deck, starting with the galley, which was roomier than Flynn expected.

"The refrigerator is more like a cooler." Herman gestured to a rectangular box the size of a mini fridge built into the counter. "So, be judicious with how often you open it. But you'll find that it's fully stocked."

Sage pulled back the lid to take a peek inside. Her eyes widened, and she quickly slammed it shut, her cheeks tinged pink.

"What's on the menu?" Flynn inched closer, curious to see what had caused her strange reaction.

"Nothing." Sage hovered in front of the fridge like a protective mama bear guarding her cubs.

"Let me have a look."

"We shouldn't open it. We need to conserve the cold temperature." Her voice had gone up an octave.

What had Mackensie put in the cooler? "I'll just take a quick peek."

Her shoulders slumped in resignation, and she begrudgingly stepped aside.

Flynn cracked open the lid. What in the world? He did a double take, making sure his mind wasn't playing tricks on him. "Is this some kind of joke?"

"I don't know what you mean, sir." Herman looked about as innocent as a criminal caught in the act.

"Why is our fridge stocked with oysters, caviar, chocolate-covered strawberries, heart-shaped crème brûlée, and three bottles of champagne?"

"Sounds like a lovely meal, sir."

"Yeah, for newlyweds."

At his comment, Sage made the unmistakable sound of someone choking on their own horror. Not that he blamed her. They'd planned on marriage once. But now? She'd probably marry a Sasquatch with smelly feet before him. Why did the realization create a gaping hole in his stomach?

"What kind of game is Mackensie playing?" he asked.

"No game, sir. Mr. Mackensie simply has very fine tastes."

"Sure." Flynn wasn't convinced the kooky billionaire didn't have ulterior motives for his culinary choices. Maybe the guy got a kick out of toying with estranged exes? The entire town knew about his breakup with Sage—the way he'd behaved like a deplorable jerk, ditching her without an explanation. Not that they knew his reasons, as if that would matter. Did Mackensie want to see him squirm?

He glanced around the galley, searching for hidden cameras while Herman highlighted the four-burner, gimbaled stove.

"Now, let's move to the main living quarters," Herman announced with a grand sweeping gesture. "Mrs. Mackensie wanted an open feel, so she had the main salon and captain's quarters combined into one large space."

They followed Herman to the back of the boat and into a long, surprisingly airy room. The black walnut trim and beams gleamed against white bulkheads, embodying a classic Herreshoff interior. Custom-built bookcases surrounded them on all sides, interspersed with booth-style seating in a rich hunter green leather.

Flynn did a 360 turn, overcome with an unexpected surge of awe and admiration. Although he knew all the exclusive and expensive brands, he didn't usually care about superficial things like fancy throw pillows or pricey paperweights. His mother had hired a designer to decorate both his penthouse apartment and his office, and he'd honestly been happy to offload the task. Even as a kid, his bedroom decor had been handpicked by a professional.

But something about this space—the combination of elegance and subtle masculinity—stirred an emotional response he hadn't expected. It felt... *homey*. Was that the right word? He wasn't sure. Nothing had felt like home before.

He glanced at Sage, wondering if she had the same impression.

Sage covered her mouth with both hands, tears glistening in her eyes. Her entire being radiated joy, wonder, and disbelief, as if she'd been lost in a desert and stumbled upon a life-saving oasis. She clearly had a connection to this place, something deep and profound. Something he didn't understand.

But one thing was undeniably apparent in her raw, vulnerable expression. Sage wanted this boat. Perhaps more than anything she'd ever wanted before.

And if he fulfilled his promise to his brother, he'd have to take it from her.

He'd broken her heart once. How could he do it again?

Chapter 14

SAGE

FOR A MOMENT, Sage couldn't move. Happiness rippled through her, making her whole body tingle. The idea to open her bookstore on a boat had been plan B. A last-ditch effort to make her dream come true. She'd never imagined something so exquisite, like stepping back in time to a world filled with elegance, grace, and beauty. Each detail—from the intricate molding to the dark, gleaming wood to the sparkling brass fixtures—radiated a regalness she hadn't expected.

Her mind instantly flooded with visions of themed book clubs, swanky meet-the-author events, even posh private parties. She could transform both the upper and lower decks into a whimsical wonderland of literature and luxury. But not the over-the-top opulence Cordelia Cahill paraded around town to make others feel less than. She wanted each person who entered her bookstore to feel special, like royalty in their own kingdom of story and imagination.

She smiled, thinking of her favorite childhood book, *The Curious Quest of Quinley Culpepper*. Oh, how she'd longed to be the heroine, Quinley, heading off on one adventure after another. Even at twelve years old, Quinley had no fear, no hesitation. She epitomized bravery and self-reliance. Qualities Sage sorely lacked. Until now.

"I gather the quarters are to your liking?" Herman asked. "Mr. Mackensie took great care to have the interior cleaned and polished."

"Everything is perfect," Sage whispered, overcome with a sense of reverence.

Until her gaze landed on the large queen bed at the back of the room. Her breath lodged in her throat, and she coughed, desperate for air as heat crept up her neck.

"Perfect, huh?" Flynn's lips twitched, and her blush deepened.

"Obviously, apart from the sleeping arrangements." An image of Flynn's tall, athletic frame splayed lazily across the plush white duvet flashed in her mind.

Get out, get out, get out.

She tried to scold the unpleasant mental image from her subconscious to no avail. Now, Imaginary Flynn had his shirt slightly unbuttoned. Her cheeks flamed, rivaling two burning coals glowing in the moonlight. There might as well be the words *Sage Harper wants to cuddle with Flynn Cahill* emblazoned on her forehead.

Except, she didn't want to be anywhere near him. If only her heart, body, and brain could get on the same page.

"What about the crew quarters?" Flynn asked Herman. "Mira didn't sail this puppy all on her own."

"The crew slept in a custom berth above deck that was, sadly, damaged during the shipwreck. Mr. Mackensie had it removed for safety reasons."

"And with all his forethought and planning over the last

two days, the guy couldn't whip up an extra bed?" Flynn asked dryly.

"Even a man of great brilliance can't think of everything."

Flynn mumbled "Uh-huh" under his breath, as if he wasn't buying Herman's answer, but Sage kept quiet. Edwin Mackensie had gone above and beyond to clean and restore a boat he planned to practically give away. *If* they could find his wife's diary. She wasn't about to complain. Even if the man's methods were more than a bit suspect. Caviar and oysters? What was *that* all about?

"We'll figure something out." She offered Herman a smile. "Thank you for the tour. If it's okay, I'd like to start looking for the diary before we lose any more daylight." Soft rays of sun streamed through round portholes and the butterfly hatches overhead, illuminating the space with bright natural light. But, according to Herman, as soon as night fell, they could dispel the darkness only with lanterns and candlelight.

"Of course. I'll bid you adieu." Herman gave a little bow in farewell and excused himself, leaving Sage alone with Flynn and his dog. The latter had already made himself at home on a long leather bench.

In Herman's absence, silence stretched between them, dulled only by the lapping of waves and occasional seagull cry.

"So, how do you wanna do this?" Flynn asked, glancing toward the bed.

Her skin sizzled again. *Stupid hormones*. "Do what?"

"This." He swung his arms to encompass the room. "We

have three days to find this thing. And I don't think you want to be on top of each other the whole time."

Another full-body hot flash swept over her. *Good grief. Get it together.* "Of course I don't," she snapped, then reeled herself in. *She who doth protest too much.* "Why don't we split the boat in two sections? We can take turns searching the different areas."

"Works for me. Do you want top or bottom first?"

"Um." She bit her lower lip, struggling to decide. Was she the only one finding it impossible to think straight? She loathed this man with every fiber of her being. So why did her traitorous stomach still spin whenever he looked at her with those sultry amber eyes as deep and dark as buckwheat honey? "I'll take below deck."

"Fine by me. Cap and I will take topside."

Sage felt a prick of hesitation at how readily he agreed. Below deck was the better choice. Unless Flynn knew that and assumed it had already been thoroughly searched in Mackensie's previous attempts to find the diary. Did she need to expand her strategy beyond the most obvious?

Anxiety fluttered in her chest like a trapped honeybee, furiously beating its wings. She couldn't lose this boat. Not to Flynn. Not to anyone. She needed a plan. She needed to get inside Mira's head.

On any given occasion, Mackensie's wife would have at least one crew member—usually two—help her man the boat. If she wanted to ensure her privacy, where would she keep her diary that was both safe but also accessible?

Her mind whirred with possibilities. Perhaps a secret compartment in one of the bookcases? She turned to find

Flynn rummaging through the bedside storage. "Excuse me? Didn't we just agree I would search below deck first?"

"Yes, thanks for the reminder." He tugged two nautical-themed quilts from the cupboard. "But unless you want to share the bed with me and Cap—who snores, by the way—I'd better borrow these."

"Oh. Right." He was letting her have the bed? Without even flipping a coin? "Where are you taking them?"

"I thought we'd sleep under the stars tonight. It's been a while since I've camped out."

She chewed her bottom lip, surprised by the twinge of guilt. Sleeping above deck would be uncomfortable. But she'd rather live with the guilt of Flynn tossing and turning all night than the alternative—sharing the same sleeping space. "Here." She grabbed one of the pillows off the bed. "Take this, too."

"Thanks." He tucked it under his arm and headed toward the companionway. "C'mon, Cap. Let's go, buddy." Flynn paused, turning to face her. "Hey. I brought two steak sandwiches for me and Cap for lunch. I've been craving Steam Engine Sammies since I got back to town. You're welcome to join us. In case you don't feel like eating oysters and caviar for the next three days."

Sage blinked, startled by the unexpected offer. Had he lost his mind? Surely he knew he was the last person she wanted as a lunch companion. "Thank you, but I brought a few snacks of my own. It's probably best if we each keep to ourselves."

"Yeah, sure. Of course." For the first time since they'd stepped on board, Flynn looked off-kilter.

Good. She shouldn't be the only one out of sorts.

"Happy hunting." He gave a little salute. "May the best man win."

"I will." As she watched him disappear through the hatch, her heart ached with an unsettling intensity.

Sure, she'd loved him once. Deeply. But that was a long time ago. And after what he'd done, she shouldn't want anything to do with him, let alone yearn to be near him as soon as he walked away.

She thought of all the women who came to the Honeybee Retreat hoping for a place to heal. Eventually, they all went home, happier and healthier. They'd learned to let go of the past, of what they'd lost. Why couldn't she do the same?

She roughly wiped a stray tear from the corner of her eye. She was being ridiculous. Strong, independent women didn't grieve a broken heart a decade old.

She'd let men like Flynn and her father live inside her head for too long.

It was time she stopped simply admiring characters like Quinley Culpepper.

She needed to *be* Quinley Culpepper.

And she'd start right here, right now. By finding that diary.

Chapter 15

LOGAN

LOGAN'S CHEST expanded with an emotion he couldn't explain as Abby bent over Max's bedside and kissed him good-night. Was it love? Happiness? Awe? All of the above? He wasn't sure. But he could stay here forever, cocooned in Max's room with the two people he cared about most in the world.

There had been a time—after the accident that left him paralyzed—when he wasn't sure he'd ever have a family. Especially when his fiancée dumped him, claiming she wasn't cut out to be with "someone like him." He'd been gutted but couldn't say he'd blamed her. He hadn't felt worthy of her love, anyway. Even after he'd learned to walk again, his self-worth hadn't returned.

It wasn't until he met Abby that he realized his character mattered far more than his physical capabilities. When it came to letting go of his stubborn pride, he still had work to do, but Abby made him want to do better. To *be* better.

She flashed him a smile as she slipped out of the room, leaving him to complete the bedtime routine—a few more chapters from *The Lion, the Witch and the Wardrobe*, followed by nightly prayers.

Even at eight years old, when some kids might resist the ritual, Max soaked up the time together. Perhaps because he'd lost his parents so young.

Logan still remembered the day his parents died. The day his faith, joy, and childlike wonder withered before his eyes. He'd been almost as old as Max. And he'd had to grow up way too fast.

How much longer until Max insisted on being too old to be tucked in? How much longer until moments like this one became nothing but a memory?

Logan tugged on the collar of his T-shirt. It suddenly felt too tight. He didn't want to think about losing Max, either to his biological father, if he ever returned, or to the natural progression of growing older.

For now, he'd focus on cherishing whatever time he had left.

"Ready to find out what happens next?" He sat on the edge of Max's bed and cracked open the well-worn book to where they'd left off the night before.

"Yeah!" Max cheered, nestled against a mound of pillows. "Can Tyler read with us, too?"

Logan's heart warmed. What a sweet kid. Tyler had arrived only yesterday, but Max had already taken the boy under his wing, looking out for him like a big brother. Despite all Max had been through—losing his mother as an infant, his father's disappearance, enduring crummy foster parents—he had a better outlook on life than most adults. He could easily be jaded and mistrusting, and yet, he genuinely cared about other people with a maturity far beyond his years.

"That's a nice thought, bud, but I think Tyler is already asleep. Maybe we can ask his mom tomorrow night?"

"Okay. And maybe she can read with us, too. It might cheer her up."

Logan furrowed his brow at the unexpected comment. "What makes you think she needs cheering up?"

"Because she was crying."

Logan's pulse kicked up a notch. Why was Piper crying? And why had Max witnessed it? He struggled to imagine an appropriate scenario for Piper to cry in front of Max. "When was this?"

"Today. After school."

"What happened?" Logan kept his tone even, but warning bells blared. Was this some sort of shady manipulation tactic? Ensnare the sympathy of their kid?

"I went upstairs to see if Tyler wanted to play. She was in the hallway, coming out of the bathroom. Her eyes were all red and stuff. And she wiped her nose with a Kleenex, but she doesn't have a cold or anything."

"I see. Did she say anything to you about why she was crying?"

"No, she just said hi. I asked her if Tyler could come outside and play. She said yes, but after his bath. I waited for him in the backyard *for-e-ver*. My baths never take that long."

"That's because you holler to get out after five minutes," Logan teased. Who knew convincing a kid to bathe would take the skills of an expert negotiator. "Maybe Tyler likes taking baths."

Max shook his head. "He doesn't. He said the best thing about car camping is not having to take a bath."

"Car camping?" Logan's thoughts flew to the jumble of belongings in the back seat of Piper's Jeep, and his pulse spiked with adrenaline.

"Yeah. He said that's what his mom calls it. It sounds fun. Except for going to the bathroom at gas stations. Those are gross." Max made a face.

Logan kept his cool, despite his knotted stomach. He'd been right. They *were* living out of their car. But why?

His heart cinched at the thought of Piper and Tyler trekking into gas station restrooms, day after day. Piper may not be his favorite person, but he had to do something about their situation. "Did Tyler say anything else about car camping?"

"Not really. Just that he likes it better here with us." Max sank deeper into the pillows and drew the blanket up to his chin. "How long are they staying?"

"I don't know, bud." They should receive the test results in a few days. Then what? Piper's charade would be blown to smithereens.

"I hope they can stay a long time," Max said with child-like innocence. "I like Tyler."

"I like him, too."

They shifted focus back to their book, but Logan struggled to concentrate. In between magic wardrobes and talking animals, his thoughts wandered to Piper and Tyler. He'd have to tell Abby what he learned from Max. But would she want to help the woman who'd stomped all over her husband's memory?

Even as the question entered his mind, he knew the

RACHAEL BLOOME

answer. Abby was the kindest person he'd ever met. A quality he admired, even on occasions like tonight, when her loving nature would put her in a difficult position.

After they'd finished their bedtime reading and moved on to their nightly prayers, Logan added a silent one for Abby. Then, with Max tucked in and drifting off to sleep, Logan joined her on the back patio.

Abby slouched in the wicker love seat, her heels propped on the edge of the brick firepit. The stillness of night surrounded her in silence, save for the crackling embers and soothing lull of the ocean waves below the bluff.

Even in the dim glow of the amber flames, worry lines etched her features, and weariness slumped her slight frame as she gazed listlessly at the moonlit waters.

Logan's gut wrenched. Despite her brave face, the last couple days had taken a toll. He not only felt helpless to fix the problem, he'd be adding to her burden. Maybe he shouldn't tell her about what he'd learned from Max? But would acting on his own to help Piper make things worse?

A stick snapped beneath his boot, and Abby turned, attempting a smile when she spotted him.

"Hey," she said softly. "How did story time go?"

"Great." The wicker creaked as he settled his weight beside her.

She instantly leaned against him, as if being close had become an instinctual habit, as if she drew strength from his presence. Oh, how he wanted that to be true. For the rest of his life, he wanted to be her main source of support.

He draped an arm around her, melting the moment she rested her head on his shoulder. Her familiar lilac scent mingled with the smoky aroma of smoldering logs, and he took a moment to savor the smell, solidifying the memory.

"I'm worried about Tyler." Her confession sliced through the comfortable silence. "I overheard Piper on the phone this morning. She said something about money and needing more time. I think they're in some kind of trouble."

Logan gathered a breath. So much for his internal debate. He had to tell her what he knew. "I think you're right." He relayed what Max shared about Tyler's car camping comments, and Abby listened, tears glistening in her hazel eyes.

"How awful," she whispered. "Poor Tyler. And Piper. I can't imagine what she's going through. As a mom, that must be terrifying." She wiped her damp cheek with the back of her hand, and Logan pulled her closer, squeezing her arm for comfort. While he hated to see her cry, he loved her tender heart.

"What do you think happened to them?" she asked.

"I have no idea." The internet search of Piper's name hadn't revealed anything useful. Except that she'd lived in Blessings Bay and tended bar at the Sawmill during the time frame she'd claimed. She wasn't on any social media sites as far as he could find, which made his sleuthing efforts even more difficult.

"Well, we have to do something to help them," Abby said with compassionate conviction.

Logan grinned despite the somber mood. Man, he loved this woman. "I knew you were going to say that. No matter what Piper has put you through, you can't resist helping someone in need."

Maybe it was the warmth of the firelight, but he thought

he detected a faint tinge to her cheeks. "Well, neither can you."

"Touché. Although, I don't have any bright ideas yet."

"I might have one. Or, it might be the worst idea I've ever had. Either way, it'll take a miracle to work."

"Luckily, Blessings Bay is kinda famous for those," he teased.

She tilted her head to meet his gaze, her perfect lips arched in the most kissable smile.

How was it possible that, with Abby, even when they found themselves in the bleakest of situations, he was exactly where he wanted to be?

SAGE

SAGE SCRUNCHED her eyes shut and yanked the covers over her head, blocking out the early morning sunlight. And the even more upsetting reality that she'd rather be anywhere else than stuck on this sailboat—with Flynn.

She would need a miracle to make it through the next few days. What made her think she could handle being this close to him again? She groaned as the gentle pressure along her temples increased to a dull percussion.

Great. A headache. Just what she needed after lying awake all night, tortured by bitter memories.

She ran a finger below her lash line and winced. Her skin felt puffy and tender to the touch, courtesy of her countless tears. She'd promised herself she wouldn't cry. She'd worked through these emotions years ago.

Except, the second she closed her eyes last night, and her body relaxed with the soothing sway of the sailboat, her thoughts betrayed her. No matter how hard she tried, she couldn't stop thinking about Kevin, Flynn, and their three-week postgraduation sailing adventure. The trip they'd spent months planning. It was supposed to be a last hurrah before she and Kevin went to college and Flynn joined the professional regatta team. Then Kevin died, and the trip became a memorial voyage in his honor. At least, that had been her hope. Flynn had agreed, at first. But something changed. The day they were supposed to set sail, he never showed. To this day, she didn't know why.

"Go away, go away, go away!" she pleaded under her breath, shooing the plaguing thoughts from her mind.

Dwelling on the past wouldn't get her anywhere. Unless it propelled her off the boat and away from Flynn, which wasn't an option. She needed to find the diary, and after her failed efforts yesterday, she had only two days left.

Focus, Sage. You can't afford a distraction if you want to—oof!

A heavy weight landed on her stomach, knocking the air from her lungs.

She jerked the covers off her head, coming face-to-drooling-face with Flynn's dog.

The excited bundle of energy wiggled his backside, pawing her arm for attention.

"Well, good morning to you, too." She chuckled and sat up to scratch behind his ears.

The contented pup flopped across her lap, soaking up the affection.

"Sorry about that. Cap took off before I could stop him." Flynn ducked through the doorway, cradling two mugs of coffee.

Sage's free hand shot to her hair. She could only imagine the tangled mess of unkempt curls. Thank goodness she'd opted to bring her matching pajama set, not her ratty T-shirt. *Wait.* Why did she care how she looked?

"Peace offering on behalf of this scalawag?" Flynn— who'd already dressed for the day in nautical board shorts and a white tee—offered her the mug. Aromatic steam filled the room with the familiar flavor notes of chocolate and nutmeg.

Her mouth watered. "Is that from CeCe's?"

"As if I'd drink any other coffee while I'm in town."

Sage rubbed Cap's neck while she contemplated Flynn's offer. The caffeine would probably help her headache. And make her feel more human. But maybe she should keep her distance and make her own?

"Take it before it gets cold." Flynn strode toward the bed and set the mug on the narrow built-in nightstand. "Don't worry. I won't get the wrong idea. Accepting the peace offering doesn't change the fact that you still hate my guts."

His eyes held a mischievous glint, and she couldn't help a smile, although she hid it behind a sip of coffee. Strong with a splash of cream. He remembered. She cleared her throat. "Good. As long as that's clear."

"Crystal." He saluted her like a naval officer. "And speaking of crystal, how would you like the fanciest breakfast of your life? I found a way to use all that date-night dinner food Edwin left us. I'm making avocado toast sprinkled with caviar, an oyster omelet with chopped scallions and chili sauce, and sauteed spinach on the side so we get our daily dose of leafy greens."

He grinned, and Sage's stomach growled. *Traitor.*

Flynn had always been gifted in the kitchen, unlike her inability to fry an egg without scorching the pan beyond recognition. But eating breakfast together? That would be a step too far. "Thanks, but I think I'll stick with coffee. Oysters upset my stomach."

"Are you talking about that time in sixth grade?" Flynn flashed an impish smile, and Sage blushed. Why had she mentioned the oysters? Ugh. So embarrassing.

She sipped her coffee instead of answering. Maybe he'd drop the subject if she ignored him.

No such luck.

"You only threw up because you had *five* fried oyster tacos then rode the merry-go-round six times in a row." He chuckled, his features softening as if he'd traveled back in time to happier days.

The sound of his laughter tugged on her heartstrings, pulling her along with him. She could almost feel the warm sun on her face and hear the cheerful music flooding the pier. "I can't believe I barfed all over Kevin's brand-new Prada loafers. He was so proud of those shoes." Her own laughter bubbled to the surface, spilling out of her unrestrained, cleansing last night's tears.

For a moment, she forgot their feud. Flynn's gaze held hers, open and unwavering—*inviting*. Something shifted between them, like a protective barrier lifting, and she didn't fight against it.

"I thought he was going to faint from horror," she admitted, sinking deeper into the memory before it slipped away. "Until you told him that in some cultures, oysters are a sign of good fortune."

"Then he went back to the taco stand and bought three more!"

They laughed together until tears trickled down their

faces. Her cheeks hurt from smiling so wide, but she didn't care. She couldn't remember the last time thoughts of Kevin had evoked anything other than pain. It actually felt good to laugh... with Flynn. She'd give anything to go back to the days before Kevin died. Before everything fell apart.

Their eyes locked again, and Sage's heart lurched. His gaze was too deep, too intimate. Heat blazed through her, setting every nerve ending on edge.

Look away. Look away now.

Her brain screamed at her, but her body wouldn't listen.

She felt herself falling, spiraling, losing control. She wanted to forget what he'd done, who he'd become. But her heart squeezed, snapping her back to the present. To the real world.

"Humorous as it was," she said, glancing away, "I'll pass on the breakfast offer. I don't think I can ever trust oysters again."

"Fair enough." His clipped tone carried all the coldness of his hurt and disappointment, as if he knew she wasn't talking about the oysters.

In an instant, the invisible door closed, slamming shut with a deafening clang.

Hopefully, for the very last time.

Chapter 17

FLYNN

FLYNN GULPED HIS COFFEE, grimacing as the hot liquid burned his throat.

"Way to go, bud. Way to stick with the plan." He shot Cap a stern look, although he wasn't entirely to blame. "We were supposed to keep to ourselves."

Unconcerned, Cap hopped back onto the bed Sage had vacated several minutes earlier to begin her search above deck. The scruffy rapscallion turned in three circles before collapsing onto the comforter with a contented huff.

"Sure, take a load off. I'll search for the diary by myself," Flynn teased. Except, he didn't move from where he stood. He couldn't tear his gaze from the soft, inviting bed.

Sage had slept between those sheets last night. Those very pillows had cushioned her head. They probably still carried the sweet, honeyed scent of her shampoo.

The tantalizing vision of her perfect body stretched beneath the covers sent his pulse sailing into dangerous waters. He shook the mental image aside. Although, it took a few minutes for his overactive heart rate to get its act together.

Had she been able to sleep last night? Her eyes looked a little red and puffy, as if she'd been crying. Did it have anything to do with him? With Kevin? Their complicated past? Or something else entirely?

The urge to comfort her, to be the one she leaned on in times of need, still permeated his being, like the impulse lived in his DNA. But he'd given up that role the day he'd betrayed her trust.

Oysters. He might not always be great at picking up on subtleties, but this time, the subtext practically screamed at him.

Why had he invited her to breakfast, anyway? Was he a glutton for punishment? Being with Sage was like some kind of exquisite torture—he needed to be near her even though her presence evoked a parade of regrets.

Last night, he'd lain awake, staring up at the stars as vast and innumerable as all the dreams he'd buried in his past. Dreams of his life with Sage, of sailing around the world on a professional regatta team, of eventually settling back in Blessings Bay to raise their three kids. Two girls and a boy. Sage had wanted to name the eldest girl Quinley after a character from her favorite book. He'd agreed to the offbeat name because, back then, he would've agreed to live on Mars if she'd asked him.

He thought of the last request she'd made—the night his brother died—and a sharp pang gripped his chest. The pain moved north, pricking the backs of his eyes. He blinked furiously and gritted his teeth, burying the memory deep in the bottomless pit of his mind where it belonged.

"All right, Cap. We gotta find this diary and get out of here." He turned a full 360, scanning the room. "If you were some lady's diary, where would you be?"

Cap lifted his bushy eyebrows but didn't budge to help.

"Please, don't get up." Rolling his eyes, Flynn strode to the nightstand, which seemed like the most logical location. Maybe it had a false bottom drawer or secret compartment?

Sage's satchel purse rested on top. He grinned at the quirky style. Multipatterned patchwork with tassels. Fun colors with a vintage, bohemian vibe. Definitely not a designer brand. A single glimpse of the faded fabric would make his mother recoil.

Beside the purse sat a worn book without a cover. A few smudges marred the cream-colored paper. But even without a proper binding, Flynn knew the title by heart.

The Curious Quest of Quinley Culpepper.

"She was nuts about this book," he told Cap, sitting on the edge of the bed. "I think it's what sparked her dream to open a bookstore." His fingers itched to feel the pages, to hold something so dear to Sage's heart.

Growing up, she'd begged him to read it, convinced every living soul on earth would benefit from its uplifting storyline about a young girl looking for her father who found her own self-worth instead. But as a kid, he hadn't wanted to invest the time in *any* book, let alone one about a twelve-year-old girl. Flynn smiled ruefully at his shortsighted younger self. He'd missed out.

Now, he owned a first edition—that had cost him more than he cared to admit—and had read it cover to cover at least a dozen times. He wasn't sure why. Some sort of self-flagellation, he supposed. He felt closer to Sage, which made his heart ache beyond reason, which led to him burying the book in the back of his closet until he dragged it out again a year later to repeat the agonizing process.

Cap nudged his hand, as if he wanted Flynn to finish the story.

"She never had a chance to open her bookstore," Flynn confessed, sadness and shame constricting his chest in equal measure.

Even after he'd left town—after he'd left Sage—he'd hoped her dream would come true. He'd felt confident it would. After all, in his estimation, she could do anything she set out to do.

He'd maintained his subscription to the *Blessings Bay Gazette*, keeping an eye out for an article on Sage and the grand opening of her bookstore. The day he'd learned his mother had opened The Best of Times—her vanity book-shop that blocked Sage from opening her own—he'd called his parents from a business trip in British Columbia. It was the one and only occasion he'd ever raised his voice to his mother.

He wasn't proud of his angry outburst—or of the subse-quent years he'd barely spoken to her—but he'd suspected her sudden interest in literature had been more spiteful than cerebral. What he didn't understand was why his mother had maintained a vendetta against a woman he'd already cut from his life.

Women—even the ones closest to him—were a mystery.

"What do you think Sage wants with *Mira*?" He scratched Cap behind his ears, surveying the room again.

Whatever the reason, he wanted her to have it. And that desire only grew the more time he spent with her—the more he felt the same indescribable, uncontrollable urge to see her smile.

Somehow, he needed to find a way to fulfill his promise to his brother *and* ensure Sage didn't lose this dream, too. Whatever this particular dream entailed.

Was dual ownership possible? Or a lease agreement?

How could he convince a woman who'd once shared her heart with him—and had it broken—to trust him with something else she valued?

ABBY

Are you sure she can be trusted with something like this?

Logan's concern echoed in Abby's mind as she approached Piper's room.

Was she sure? Not even a little bit. But what else could she do? She didn't feel comfortable handing unsolicited cash to an unscrupulous stranger. Especially one claiming to be her husband's one-night stand. But she couldn't allow this woman and her child to live in their car without trying to help in some small way, could she?

Her fist hovered half an inch from the door, poised to knock. The anxious thrum of her heartbeat filled her eardrums like the warning hum of ocean waves, luring her to safety, away from her fool's errand.

She didn't need to do this. She'd be perfectly justified to let the woman fend for herself, especially after all she'd put her through. The last two nights, she'd barely slept.

Whenever she closed her eyes, her cruel imagination tormented her thoughts. She begged her brain to stop, to let her sleep, but she couldn't dispel the visions of Donnie and Piper tangled in bed together, a mass of sweaty limbs and silken sheets.

Last night, she'd woken at 2 a.m., her cheek damp from her tearstained pillow, her stomach churning. The nightmare had felt so real, as if she'd witnessed the illicit affair with her own two eyes.

For the rest of the night until dawn, she'd lain awake, staring into the darkness, wrestling with her tumultuous emotions. If the thought of Donnie with another woman made her physically sick, what did that say about her feelings for Logan?

Abby let her arm drop to her side.

The spacious hallway suddenly closed in around her, and she struggled to breathe as the once pleasant scent of lemon polish and fresh flowers now felt suffocating.

She loved Logan. Wholly and completely. But her love for Donnie hadn't disappeared. Their marriage—what they'd shared—would always hold a special place in her heart. And Piper had trampled all over it.

Hot tears stung her eyes, and she blinked furiously, biting back a sob of frustration. This needed to end. The constant pain and confusion. The battle between compassion for Piper's situation and her visceral dislike for the woman. She couldn't take it anymore.

Abby turned, ready to leave, when the door to Piper's room cracked open.

Tyler gazed up at her, one chubby little hand on the doorknob, his angelic face glowing with the brightest grin. "Hi, Miss Abby!"

Suppressing her tears, she summoned a smile. "Hi, Tyler."

"Is Max home from school yet?"

"Not yet."

"Okay." Tyler sighed but maintained his smile, as if he had plenty of practice dealing with disappointment.

Abby's thoughts flew to what Logan shared last night. Tyler, asleep in the back of Piper's Jeep. Tyler, trekking into gas station restrooms to brush his teeth. Tyler, living off granola bars and bottled water.

A lump lodged in her throat, and try as she might, she couldn't will it away. "May I speak to your mom for a minute?"

"Yeah! She's on the balcony, but I'll go get her." He scampered back into the room, and Abby waited, her stomach tangled in knots.

Piper came to the door, her stiff stance wary and guarded. "Yes?" Her gaze briefly dropped to Abby's hands, as if she expected her to be holding something. The test results? At the sight of Abby empty-handed, a flicker of disappointment flashed in her eyes.

Abby swallowed. Her mouth had gone unpleasantly dry. "I—" She hesitated, nearly losing her nerve. *Think of Tyler.* "I was wondering if you'd do me a favor." She forced herself to meet Piper's gaze.

"What?" Piper's eyes widened.

"I—I could use an extra set of hands around the inn." She curled her fingers into her palms to fend off the slight tremor. "I have incredibly important guests arriving soon, and I could use some additional help. Light housekeeping, coordinating activities, running errands. That kind of thing."

Piper could help anywhere but in the kitchen. That was her sacred space.

"You're serious?"

"I can pay you two hundred dollars a day."

"Two hundred dollars?" Piper repeated, as if she couldn't quite believe what she'd heard.

"Yes. Are you interested?" Abby held her breath, half wishing Piper would decline.

Piper kneaded her bottom lip, glancing over her shoulder at her son. Tyler sat on the bed flipping through the pages of a picture book. "I—I don't know."

"I realize it might be a little awkward, but it's only for a few days." She refrained from adding *until the test results arrive*, and said, "We can work in different parts of the house. I doubt we'll see each other any more than we do right now."

This seemed to assuage some of her concerns, but she still looked reticent. "What about Tyler?"

"I don't mind if he tags along while you work. But he's also welcome to hang out with Verna. I've already spoken with her, and she'd love to spend time with him. She's like a surrogate grandma to Max."

"She does seem great with kids, but I still don't know if it's a good idea."

Abby bit her tongue. She wanted to help Piper for Tyler's sake, but she refused to beg.

"I guess I can help you out," Piper relented, as if she was doing Abby a huge personal favor.

"Great." Abby ignored Piper's ingratiating tone. "When can you start?"

"Right now, if Verna's free. Let me talk to Tyler first.

We'll be down in a sec." Without another word, Piper closed the door in her face.

The resounding click echoed in the hall with an ominous note of finality.

A tiny tingle of misgiving tickled Abby's throat.

Had she just made a horrible mistake?

Chapter 19

ABBY

"HAVE YOU LOST YOUR MIND?" Nadia Chopra hissed. Her dark eyes narrowed, following Piper as she dusted the fireplace mantel on the other side of the sitting room. Thanks to her earbuds, Piper appeared oblivious to their conversation. "First, you let her stay in your inn, free of charge. Then, you *hire* her. Do I need to organize some kind of intervention?"

"It's not like I offered her a full-time position. It's only for a few days. And you know why I had to do it." She'd explained the situation when Nadia arrived to help assemble the welcome baskets for Sadie and Lucy, who were expected in two days.

"Well, *had* to might be a stretch. But yes, it's a sad situation. I'm not unsympathetic. But there are a million ways this scenario could end badly. If you need help, I have time."

"No, you don't. You're busy building your empire. And I couldn't be prouder."

In a few short months, her brilliant friend had turned her boyfriend's rash balm into a rapidly growing business. By marketing Epic Inc. as an active and adventurous lifestyle brand, she'd already made endorsement deals with several social media influencers. Not only for Evan's rash balm, but also his latest product—a sensational new body scrub that Nadia generously agreed to include in Abby's welcome baskets, even before its official debut.

"I always have time for you," Nadia assured her. "Especially if it keeps you from hiring Piper. I don't trust a woman who doesn't wear mascara."

Abby smiled at her effortlessly stylish friend. "Nadia, *I'm* not wearing mascara."

"You're not?" Nadia swept a strand of silky black hair away from her eyes and peered closer. "Wow. You have fabulous lashes. Okay, I retract my former statement. But makeup aside, I don't trust her."

"I don't, either. But it's not like I gave her the password to my bank account. She's *dusting*. What's the worst that could happen?" Abby tried to sound self-assured despite her own misgivings.

A shadow crossed Nadia's features, and her gaze fell to the gift baskets. Although, she didn't seem to register the scented soaps, body scrubs, and gourmet sweets nestled inside.

Abby's pulse quickened during the agonizingly long pause. What was her friend struggling to say? Nadia never had trouble speaking her mind.

Finally, Nadia lifted her gaze. "Abs," she said softly, her expression pained. "Is there any chance Piper is telling the truth?"

The weighted question swung through the air like a wrecking ball, both necessary yet gut-wrenching.

Abby winced. Not that she blamed Nadia for asking. Nadia's ex, Brian, had been Donnie's best friend—both test pilots at Edwards Air Force Base with a shared passion for speed and adrenaline. And, Abby once thought, for duty and honor.

Last New Year's Eve, Nadia uncovered Brian's affair the same night he proposed. She'd gone from being engaged to publicly devastated before the ball had fully dropped in Times Square.

Of course Nadia had reason to suspect Donnie of cheating. She'd learned firsthand that sometimes it's the people you least suspect who can hurt you the most.

But Donnie wasn't like Brian. Brian may have won Nadia over, but she'd never trusted him. He was too slick, like a shiny, slippery surface primed for a fall. Whereas she'd entrusted her very life to Donnie without hesitation. And that had included her heart.

"No. It's not possible." The slight waver in her voice betrayed her tiny sliver of doubt. She focused on fluffing the turquoise bow tied to the basket's wicker handle, avoiding Nadia's gaze.

"I'm sure you're right. But all the same, when was the last time you went over your finances?"

"I just purchased a new accounting program." It was her second big investment after online reservation software. But from the frown on Nadia's face, it wasn't the answer she wanted.

A cold shiver swept through her. *Please, don't bring up Donnie's money*, she silently pleaded. *Not again.*

She knew her friend meant well. After Donnie's accident, Nadia had encouraged her to get a handle on his finances, life insurance, and military benefits. It made perfect sense. It was the mature, responsible thing to do. But Abby couldn't bring herself to touch Donnie's money. Or his secret beach house in Blessings Bay—the house that had become her home—until she'd been desperate for a secluded escape last Christmas.

She'd tried to rationalize her reticence, to explain why she'd left every dime sitting in his separate bank account. But denial that deep didn't make sense until you lost someone so important—so closely entwined with your own heart and soul—that merely acknowledging their absence stole your breath away.

Until Nadia felt a similar loss—heaven forbid—she'd never understand.

"You know what I meant," Nadia pressed, her direct tone tempered with kindness. "And from your avoidance, I assume you're still letting Donnie's lawyer handle everything?"

Abby fussed with the bow. Why couldn't she get the loops even? *Ugh.* She yanked the ribbon, undoing the bow altogether.

"Abs." Nadia's voice crept across the table. "It's been over a year since Donnie died. Don't you think it's time to do something with all that money? To finally put it to good use?"

Abby crumpled the ribbon into a ball, crinkling the smooth satin. Talking about Donnie's money left a hollow void in her stomach. She'd thought about emptying his accounts before. She could invest the money in her business. Or donate it all to a worthy cause. But for some reason, she couldn't make a decision. It felt too... *final*.

"Maybe." She shrugged. "But I don't need it. I have savings. And the inn is doing well." For the first time in her life, she felt proud of her own accomplishment. She wasn't merely supporting someone else's passion. She had her own goals and dreams.

"The inn is amazing," Nadia agreed. "But..." She trailed off, as if searching for the right word.

Abby's muscles tensed. For the second time in one conversation, her typically candid friend seemed hesitant.

Nadia cast a furtive glance at Piper, who'd moved into the foyer to dust the vintage hall stand. Turning back to Abby, she said, "I think it would be wise to call Donnie's lawyer. Have him send you all the financials. I can go over them with you, if that helps. But you should at least be informed. Then, once you know all the numbers, you can decide what to do with it all. Okay?"

Abby nodded slowly, staring at the limp, wrinkled ribbon in her hand as an icy dread clamped around her heart.

An ominous, unspoken implication hid behind Nadia's simple request.

If the paternity results came back positive, Piper and her son would be entitled to a portion of everything she owned.

And it would behoove her to know exactly how much she had at stake.

As if losing her faith in Donnie—in their marriage—wasn't bad enough.

Chapter 20

SAGE

WHAT AM I doing up here?

Sage clung to the wooden mast like a squirrel on a telephone pole, feeling foolish. Or desperate. Or both.

The setting sun warmed the back of her neck and arms. Sweat gathered along her hairline, but more from the mental and physical exertion than the heat. She'd been searching the deck all day, scouring every square inch for the diary. But no luck. Panic settled in her chest. She hadn't found it below deck, either, and she was running out of places to look.

Hence her ridiculous idea to search the rigging.

"Where did you hide the diary, Mira?" she whispered into the wind. "It has to be here somewhere."

A heavy knot settled in her stomach, weighing her down. She readjusted her grip. What if she never found the diary? Or what if Flynn found it? She shuddered at the thought.

For the millionth time that day, her thoughts wandered to their conversation earlier that morning. For a moment, she'd forgotten everything that happened between them. It had felt so good to laugh together. Safe. Familiar. Cathartic.

Against her will, all her feelings for Flynn came flooding back. She viscerally remembered what it felt like to love him, so wholly and trusting.

And to be loved *by* him.

Yes, they'd been mere kids. Barely eighteen when they broke up. But during their time together, he'd made her believe in herself in a way no one else had. Not even her mom or Gran. With his unwavering faith in her—and the way he looked at her as if her radiance surpassed the sun and stars— he'd soothed the wounds left by her father. Every emotional cut and bruise telling her she wasn't good enough, that she wasn't worthy of someone else's time or affection.

In his own special way, he'd given her friendship, love, and the courage to find her self-confidence—a powerful combination that made her believe anything was possible.

Brick by brick, he'd helped her rebuild what her father tore down. Then he left, and in the wake of his absence, the rubble of her broken heart surpassed all hope of repair.

A tear slid down her cheek, and she released one hand from the mast to wipe it away.

Get it together, Sage. You don't need Flynn. Or any man. You just need to find the diary and finally get on with your life.

A startling bark broke through her thoughts, and before she could catch herself, her grip slipped. She tumbled backward, hitting the hard deck with a thud.

A sharp pang shot through her ankle.

She groaned, grimacing in pain.

Cap gently nuzzled her with his nose, as if apologizing for the unintentional scare.

"It's okay." She pet the top of his head. "You're forgiven."

She tried to put a little weight on her ankle, then winced. *Great*. A sprained ankle was the last thing she needed.

"Cap? Are you up here? You're not sup—" Flynn's voice faltered the second he spotted her sprawled on the deck, nursing her ankle. Panic flickered in his eyes. He rushed over and knelt by her side. "What happened? Are you okay?"

He scanned her body for signs of injury, and she realized her long skirt had bunched around her thighs during the fall. She quickly yanked the fabric back over her legs.

"I'm fine. I just twisted my ankle." She tried to stand but wobbled, and instantly sat back down.

"Don't move. Let me take a look." He lifted the hem of her skirt a few inches and carefully cupped the curve of her ankle.

She inhaled sharply as his touch instantly shot tingles up her leg.

He traced his palm from her calf to the heel of her foot, assessing the damage.

Heat spread over her body, and she closed her eyes, trying to focus on anything other than the feel of his fingertips against her bare skin.

As he leaned over her, his heady scent tickled her nose. Citrus and ocean spray. Crisp, masculine, and painfully familiar. After all these years, why couldn't he wear a different cologne?

He must have noticed the ragged edge to her breath, because he said, "Don't worry. It doesn't look swollen or bruised. I doubt it's even a sprain. A couple of painkillers and some rest, and you'll be good as—"

When he didn't finish his sentence, she opened her eyes. She followed his gaze to her opposite ankle—the one wearing the friendship bracelet. Her heartbeat fluttered. What was he thinking? She couldn't read his cloudy expression.

He cleared his throat, adding, "Good as new." He tore his gaze from her ankle and the cloud lifted. "Don't panic or pepper spray me, but I'm going to pick you up."

"What? Why?" Despite his instruction not to panic, her pulse skyrocketed.

"Because you shouldn't put any weight on your ankle for a few hours at least."

"A few hours? Fat chance. In case you've forgotten, we're embroiled in a do-or-die competition."

He smiled at her dramatics. "Then how about a truce?"

"What kind of truce?"

"How about for the rest of the evening, neither one of us looks for the diary."

"But that would mean we'd only have tomorrow left to look for it."

He shrugged. "In the last two days, we've been over this boat a hundred times. Logically, there are only a handful of places left to look. One more day is plenty of time to find it."

She frowned. While she didn't share his optimism, she didn't want to exaggerate her injury by hobbling around on a bum ankle, either. Maybe a temporary truce was a good idea. "What's in it for you?"

"What do you mean?"

"Well, you now have an advantage. You could keep looking for the diary without me."

"That's true. I could. But between you and me, I could use a break. It's almost dinnertime, and during my search, I spotted a Daiwa Marine Power Electric Reel, and I've been dying to give it a whirl."

She raised an eyebrow. Flynn was willing to give up precious treasure-hunting time for a fancy *fishing pole*? She didn't buy his excuse for a second. Why was he being so nice to her? And why did she want to accept his offer?

"Besides," he added with an impish grin, "I don't need an unfair advantage. I'll find the diary first, fair and square."

Her stomach spun at the sight of his playful smile, the way his amber eyes lit from within, illuminating his whole face—his frustratingly handsome face. Some people really had no business being that good-looking.

"Fine. A *temporary* truce. One night only. Tomorrow morning at dawn, the search continues."

"Works for me."

Before she could say another word, he scooped her into his arms. She wanted to protest, but every objection died in her throat, silenced by the feel of his arms wrapped around her.

She resisted the urge to rest her head on his shoulder. No matter how her body responded to his nearness—to the hard contours of his chest, strong flex of his forearms, or the faint stubble on his jawline tempting her fingertips—she couldn't succumb to the false sense of security.

The temporary pain of a twisted ankle couldn't even compare to the agony of a heart broken by Flynn Cahill.

He eased her onto a deck chair, and she immediately missed his touch.

"Don't move," he instructed. "I'm going to grab the fishing pole for me and a book for you. Do you want any one in particular?"

"Surprise me." If she were honest, she'd just forgotten the

title of every book ever written. She'd never been more discombobulated in her life.

He glanced at Cap. "Keep an eye on her. Don't let her move from this spot. Got it?"

Cap dutifully sat by her side.

As she watched Flynn walk toward the companionway, her heart wrenched.

How was it possible to resent someone so deeply while simultaneously regretting every second you spent apart?

Chapter 21

FLYNN

FLYNN FLIPPED the filleted halibut on the small propane grill secured to the safety railing. The lightly seasoned skin sizzled, sending the mouthwatering aroma of seared fish into the air. Dark clouds accumulated over the mountains in the distance, but cocooned in the bay, the cool evening air blew gently, and soothing waves lapped against the boat's hull.

He stole a glance at Sage, still settled on the deck chair, a book propped open on her lap. She stroked Cap's fur with one hand and flipped the pages with the other. The setting sun bathed the idyllic scene with soft sepia tones, lending a dreamlike quality.

Is this what his life could've been like?

At the thought, regret roiled in his stomach. He'd lost a decade of happiness. Had it all been worth it?

He took a swig of cream soda, barely noticing the sweet notes of vanilla bean or the damp droplets of condensation clinging to the glass bottle. His mind reeled with what-ifs.

What if he'd never abandoned the woman he loved? The woman who amplified each sliver of life by her mere existence. He'd tried to forget her over the years. He'd implemented every distraction, exerted every effort. There were times the agony of missing her waned ever so slightly, making the memories almost bearable. *Almost.*

Then there were days like today. Days when the realization of what he'd done—what he'd given up—crushed him with so much force, he couldn't breathe.

After her fall, he'd wanted to keep an eye on her, so he'd dragged a deck chair beside hers, insisting this side of the boat had the best fishing conditions. While he wasn't convinced she'd bought his ruse entirely, she hadn't protested, either. They'd nibbled on crackers and caviar, sitting in companionable silence while he caught their dinner and Sage read her book.

He'd half expected her to decline when he placed her worn copy of *The Curious Quest of Quinley Culpepper* on her lap. A glint of surprise had flashed in her eyes, but then she'd smiled and opened the book to the first page, which she probably had memorized by now.

While she read, she occasionally broke concentration for a snack or soda break, and he'd steal the opportunity to insert a casual remark, hoping to spark some conversation. To his delight, she took the bait, and they chatted about random topics, off and on, as if their truce had somehow transcended the treasure hunt.

As if, at least temporarily, she'd forgiven him.

For those few precious hours, being together came easily, without angst or tension. He'd sunk into her presence like a dip in a healing hot spring, savoring each second, knowing it wouldn't last.

But oh, how he wished it would.

And from the way Cap soaked up her attention, he did, too.

The wind fluttered the pages of her novel, and Sage paused from petting Cap to find her spot.

"How many times have you read that book?" he asked, knowing it had to be in the double digits, at least.

"About a hundred," she confessed with a sheepish smile. "But it never gets old."

"Speaking of old." He flipped another fillet, then gestured toward the book with the spatula. "You know you can pay someone to re-cover that, right?"

"I know." She placed her finger in the spine and gingerly closed the book to admire the faded title page. "I like it this way. There's something special about an unbound book. As if the story isn't confined by a clear beginning and end. Like it exists in a universe with infinite possibilities. Even when you think it's over, it never really is. It reminds me that a good story lives forever, in our hearts and minds."

Despite the fish sizzling and blackening on the grill, he couldn't tear his gaze from Sage's face. As she spoke, her features softened, and her pale-green eyes sparkled. He'd glimpsed a similar dreamy expression the first time she went below deck, as if *Mira* and her love of literature stirred something deep and profound in her soul. As if books and this boat evoked the same sense of awe and wonder that sailing sparked in his heart.

The sudden undeniable, overwhelming urge to kiss her consumed his thoughts. His pulse quickened, and his skin prickled, itching to be near her, to feel the curve of her cheek against his palm.

He wanted to share in her passions. Her hopes. Her

dreams. In every aspect of her life. But he'd given up that right. He'd thrown it away, as if it meant nothing to him. As if the decision didn't tear his heart in two, every second of every day.

He cleared his throat. "That's a cool way to look at it."

Even when you think it's over, it never really is.

Her words echoed in his mind. Oh, how he wished she were talking about the two of them, not a work of fiction.

He scooped the crispy halibut off the grill and slid them onto a plate to cool. Cap scampered over to him and sat on his haunches, gazing up at him with round, pleading eyes, oblivious to his internal torment.

"Okay, okay. You don't have to beg." Flynn tore off a generous chunk, blew on it a few times and checked for bones, then tossed it to Cap.

The happy pup eagerly gobbled up the treat.

Flynn caught Sage observing the exchange with a curious expression. "What?" he asked. "Do you think I spoil him? Because if that's what you're thinking, you're right."

"It's not that. It's just a little strange watching you two together. I never thought of you as a dog person."

"So, you've thought about me, huh?" he teased.

"*If* I've thought about you"—she matched his playful tone—"which I'm neither confirming nor denying, there's a high probability it wasn't fondly."

"Ouch." He clutched his chest as if he'd been wounded, hamming up the humor while his gut knotted with regret. "But fair," he added with a wry grin, trying to be a good sport. He deserved every jab she threw, in jest or otherwise. "And you're right, by the way. I wasn't a dog person before Cap. I didn't have time for a dog. Or a goldfish. Or a cactus."

"What changed?" She closed the book and let it rest in her lap, not bothering to save her spot.

"It's a long story." He tossed Cap another hunk of halibut.

"Well, I'm clearly not going anywhere." She gestured to her ankle and smiled.

"True." She'd given him a free pass to share something personal, to open a window into his life. He'd be a fool not to take the opportunity. "Five years ago, I was in a business meeting in Dallas. A big merger. The guy leading the negotiation for the other side came into the conference room with this little yellow furball tucked under one arm." Flynn sank into a squat and ruffled the scruff at Cap's neck.

"He brought a puppy to a business meeting?"

"Believe me. I was as surprised as you are. He said he got the dog for his kids, but this troublemaker"—he scratched Cap behind the ears—"developed a taste for designer heels."

"Oh, no!" Sage laughed.

"The guy's wife wasn't too keen on having her Christian Louboutins turned into chew toys, so Cap had to go. She wouldn't let him back in the house, even while her husband was negotiating a multimillion-dollar merger."

"Poor Cap." At her sweet, sympathetic tone, Cap trotted back to her side, happy to double up on the affection.

Flynn stood and leaned against the railing, recalling that day's unexpected events. "So, the guy's telling me how he had no choice but to bring the so-called *bad* dog to the meeting and how he's going to dump him at the pound as soon as it's over—"

"That's awful!" Sage interrupted with adorable outrage.

She'd always had a soft spot for animals. Another trait he'd admired.

"Yeah. The guy was a real piece of work. While he droned on and on about how a *good* dog should behave, Cap figured out how to use my briefcase and a vacant chair as a stepladder onto the conference table."

"No! He didn't." Sage put a hand to her mouth, smothering another laugh.

"Yep. He was quite resourceful. And it gets better." Flynn's gaze fell on Cap, his heart warming at the memory. "I reach for my cappuccino, but the cup's empty. And this thief has a suspicious foam mustache."

"You drank your dad's cappuccino?" Sage asked Cap, who wiggled his backside in unabashed admission.

"Every last drop. I was actually kinda impressed. Both that he'd managed to get onto the conference table undetected and that he could handle a double-shot espresso."

"And that's what made you decide to keep him?" she asked with an amused smirk. "His caffeine tolerance?"

Flynn hesitated, weighing his response. He could answer her question with another joke. Or he could tell her the truth. "I decided to keep Cap because I understood him. He wasn't a bad dog. He simply needed someone who would appreciate his mischievous, playful side while helping to redirect some of his rambunctious energy with love and patience." All the things his parents never offered him.

Sage met his gaze and wordlessly communicated both empathy and understanding in a single glance. She'd witnessed all the times he'd been scolded by his parents. All the times they'd asked, *Why can't you be more like your brother?*

136

Kevin was always focused, orderly, and disciplined. He was going places. Good places. The *right* places. Kevin was the mega yacht while Flynn was the racing schooner, too difficult for his parents to control.

At least, he used to be, before Kevin died.

"Wait." Sage sat up straighter, snapping him back to the present. "Cap? As in, *Cap*puccino?"

"Yep."

"Huh." She leaned back. "And I thought it was short for Captain, because you sail so often."

Flynn shifted his body toward the sea, his forearms propped on the railing. The sun sank below the horizon, splashing pinks and yellows across the water as the sky above turned a dusty blue. He owed Sage the truth. But he couldn't reveal the whole truth. Not without hurting her even more than he already had. He drew in a breath of salty sea air, weighing his words carefully. "I haven't been sailing in years."

"Really? Why not?"

He shrugged. "No time." The knot in his stomach cinched. He hadn't lied. Not entirely. Sure, he could *make* time, if he really wanted, but it wouldn't be easy. Not with how many hours his job required. And once he became VP, his free time would shrink to nonexistent.

"I don't understand. Why do you want this boat if you don't even sail anymore?" Her tone carried a hint of exasperation mixed with confusion, and he winced.

Bracing himself, he turned to face her.

She met his gaze with wary, questioning eyes. Her posture, once relaxed, now looked tense and guarded.

She deserved answers. Answers he couldn't give her.

137

Once again, for her sake, he opted to respond with partial truths. "The boat isn't for me."

Her eyes widened, and he plunged ahead before she got the wrong idea.

"It's not a gift for a girlfriend or anything like that. I don't have a girlfriend. I don't date. I—" Heat shot up his neck. *Good grief. Get it together, man. You're babbling like a buffoon.* He gathered another breath. "The boat's for Kevin."

"Now I really don't understand." Although still cautious, her tone softened at the mention of his brother's name.

"Do you remember Kevin's bucket list?" he asked. "The one he made our senior year?"

"Of course. His 30 Before 30 list. He'd tried to convince me to make one, too."

"Did he ever show it to you?"

"No. He shared a few of the things he'd added, but not the whole thing. Why?"

Flynn reached into his back pocket and pulled out his wallet. His fingers shook slightly as he flipped open the buttery leather and slid out a slip of paper. "Here." He handed the neatly folded square to Sage, studying every inch of her expression as she slowly unfolded the sheet of monogrammed stationery and scanned the list.

At the sight of Kevin's perfect penmanship, and the thirty even rows detailing his youthful hopes and dreams, tears filled her eyes. When she finally lifted her gaze, her eyes sparkled again, but this time, not from blissful, bookish reverie. Her eyes glistened with pain and sadness.

"You're fulfilling Kevin's bucket list?"

"I've been working on it for the last ten years. I only have the last two items left."

She glanced down at the page and read them aloud. "Own the *Marvelous Mira* and become vice president of Cahill Enterprises."

"That's why I'm back in town," he confessed. "My parents are announcing my promotion at the gala tomorrow night. It's only a coincidence that I discovered *Mira* on the auction brochure."

"So all of this—" Her voice caught as her gaze swept the page again. "You're completing everything on this list in honor of Kevin's memory?"

"Something like that." He turned back toward the water. Without the sun's light, the sea darkened. Silver-tipped waves caressed the boat's hull, creating a rhythmic sway, lulling him back to the past, to memories as murky as the ocean depths.

He could still hear his mother's sobs from the day of his brother's funeral—the day he'd approached his father's study and forever changed the course of his life.

"Why him?" His mother's bitter cry had carried through the crack in the door frame.

He should've walked away right then, but he'd crept closer, peering through the gap as his pulse hammered inside his eardrums.

"Please, God," she'd pleaded, weeping against his father's chest. Her whole body shook with the force of her sobs, despite his father's arms wrapped tightly around her, his own tears tumbling down his face.

Witnessing his parents in so much anguish, Flynn had felt as though his already broken heart had been ripped from his body.

"Please, God," his mother repeated, her voice breaking. "*Please*. Anyone but our Kevin."

At that moment, time had stopped. All the air fled his lungs, as if they'd been punctured by an ice pick. He couldn't move. Or breathe. Or even think straight. All he felt was the crushing pain of her words.

And all the words she didn't say, but he already knew.

Anyone but our Kevin.

Our favorite. The son meant to carry on our legacy and esteemed Cahill name. The son who made us proud.

If he'd been given a choice that day, he would've traded places with his brother without hesitation.

But he hadn't been given a choice.

Which left him with the next best option: to try as hard as possible to fill his brother's shoes.

Burying the memory as best he could, he faced Sage once more and forced a smile. "Should we eat before the fish gets cold?"

"Sure."

He reached for the spatula, but not before he caught the look in her eyes. The look he'd seen so many times growing up, when they'd been each other's best friend. The look that said, *I'm here for you if you need to talk.*

More than anything, he wanted to invite her into this part of his life. The part he'd had to process all on his own.

But how could he tell the woman he loved—the woman he longed to protect—that she'd played an unwitting role in his brother's death?

Chapter 22

SAGE

SAGE STARED up at the obsidian sky framed by the butterfly hatch overhead. The ocean rumbled and roared, and the thick salt-slicked air hung around her like a damp curtain. *Mira* lolled from side to side, but despite the soothing motion, she couldn't sleep.

Her mind still reeled from her earlier conversation with Flynn. And the haunted glint in his eyes when he spoke about his brother's bucket list.

He'd devoted ten years to completing all thirty of Kevin's youthful ambitions. Is that why he'd left Blessings Bay? Why he'd left *her*?

She'd wanted to ask him, but the words wouldn't form past the lump of trepidation caught in her throat. What if she didn't like his answer? What if his answer confirmed what she'd long suspected? That she simply hadn't been enough for him. For all the years she'd craved closure, she wasn't sure she could bear the truth.

The last item on the list flashed into her mind. *Become vice president of Cahill Enterprises.* Kevin had lived and breathed all things business. As kids, while she and Flynn built sandcastles for pirates and princesses, Kevin constructed Cahill Tower, a commercial skyscraper with an attached parking garage made of driftwood.

Kevin was born to be VP. But Flynn? If someone had asked her ten years ago if he'd take over the family business, she would've scoffed. The old Flynn Cahill wouldn't last two seconds in a boardroom before he got bored, in the literal sense.

But now? She wasn't so sure. For the last decade, he'd lived the life Kevin always wanted. He was wealthy, successful, and highly esteemed in the business world. But she couldn't stifle the feeling that something wasn't quite right with Flynn's flawless facade. He wasn't being true to the man God created him to be, and ten years ago, she would've told him exactly how she felt.

A rogue wave slapped against the hull, rocking *Mira* to one side. Sage tumbled in the sheets, nearly toppling out of bed. She gripped the bed frame, clinging with all her might until *Mira* righted herself.

Her heart racing, she maintained her tight grasp on the frame, waiting a beat for her pulse to return to its resting rate before letting go.

The wind howled, and every inch of *Mira* creaked and groaned in response.

Were Flynn and Cap okay above deck?

Another wave assaulted *Mira*'s starboard side, and Sage scrambled to secure a safe grip as the boat lilted. Did the bed have some sort of guardrail for this kind of situation?

At the thought, she wondered, once again, how Flynn

and Cap were faring topside. Maybe she should invite them below deck until the waves calmed?

A vision of Flynn in his pajamas with sexy rumpled hair invaded her vivid imagination, sending her already racing pulse soaring.

Nope. Definitely a bad idea.

The howling wind settled to a low whistle, and the boat's violent sway simmered to a slow bob.

Maybe the worst was over?

Pitter-patter, pitter-patter...

Raindrops played a gentle percussion on *Mira*'s wood siding.

Great. Just what she needed. She couldn't leave them up there in the rain, could she?

Apprehension built in her chest. With each stumbling step she took toward the companionway, aided by the flashlight on her phone, her heart whispered a warning.

This will end in disaster.

The rain grew louder and more persistent, pelting *Mira* on all sides. The boys would be soaked by now.

A noise in the galley caught her attention, and she aimed the beam of light inside. A dripping-wet Flynn knelt by Cap's side, drying him off with dish towels.

"Sorry." Flynn winced in the harsh glare, and she tilted her phone away from his eyes. "I know we're encroaching on enemy territory, but it's dumping buckets up there."

"I was just going topside to get you." Her gaze fell to the white T-shirt plastered to his rock-solid chest. Even in the dim lighting, she could trace the outline of his contoured abs. Her cheeks heated, and she quickly averted her gaze. But not before her mouth went as dry as a sand dune.

"You were?" He cocked his head in surprise. Could he tell she was blushing?

"Okay, I was actually coming up to get Cap, but I figured he'd only agree to come down with me if you came along, too." She tried to sound breezy and casual, while inside, her heartbeat thundered as hard as the rain.

"Thanks." He stood; his features relaxed with relief. "Cap and I can throw together a makeshift bed on the floor. You'll barely even notice us." He combed his fingers through his wet hair, and the strands by his forehead curled into sexy tendrils.

Yeah, right. Her stomach swayed even more than *Mira*. She wouldn't be able to breathe with Flynn nearby, let alone sleep. And yet, the realization didn't stop her from blurting, "We can share the bed."

His eyes widened, and his slack jaw conveyed all the shock she felt.

"I—I mean," she stammered, trying to talk some sense into her traitorous hormones. Or was her heart the more likely culprit? "All three of us can share the bed. It's a queen, so there's plenty of room. You can sleep on top of the sheets, and Cap can sleep in between us."

Had she lost her mind?

The boat pitched to one side, and she braced herself against the doorjamb.

Cap barked in excitement, as if he enjoyed the amusement ride.

"Don't trust yourself, huh?" Flynn's athletic frame followed each swell and dip of the boat, matching *Mira*'s movements.

She tried not to notice the way his muscles flexed with the motion. Or the mischievous twinkle in his eyes.

"Not to shave your eyebrows in your sleep?" she teased, deflecting with humor. "No, I don't. And you shouldn't trust me, either."

He laughed, and the rich, rumbling sound made her feel more unsteady than the shifting floor beneath her feet.

Their eyes locked, and a current of heat surged between them.

He took a step toward her, but another wave struck *Mira*'s side, launching Sage forward. She met Flynn's chest with a thud, and his back slammed against the wall.

Cap barked again, having a ball as Sage's phone clattered to the floor. With the flashlight facing down, they plunged into moonlit darkness.

Flynn's chest rose and fell beneath her fingertips, his breath deep and ragged. Her fists coiled around his damp shirt, while his hands splayed across her lower back, pressing her against him.

She inhaled sharply, not daring to breathe as their bodies moved together, in time with the rhythmic waves.

"Are you okay?" His voice finally broke through the scintillating silence, strained and raspy.

She tipped her chin until their eyes met.

His gaze glowed in the darkness, fiery and intense, his desire unmistakable.

She couldn't look away.

"I—I don't know," she answered honestly, her emotions an indiscernible jumble.

He pressed harder against the small of her back, leaving

no space between them. His lips were so close, she could almost taste them.

In all her life, no one had ever kissed her like Flynn Cahill. The man kissed the same way he handled a sailboat—with passion, skill, and flawless intuition.

What would he do if she lightly pressed her lips to his? Would he stop her? And more importantly, would she want him to?

Her heart hammered its answer so loudly, it muffled the pounding rain.

At that moment, she didn't care about self-preservation.

She simply wanted to pretend. To exist in what could've been.

Let Future Sage deal with the fallout.

Chapter 23

FLYNN

FLYNN TRIED to steady his breath but failed. His entire body burned with an uncapped current of electricity. His fingers tingled against Sage's lower back, itching to slide beneath the hem of her shirt and feel her soft skin.

He'd never wanted anyone more than he wanted Sage in that moment, and his emotions warred with each other—desire against duty.

He could kiss her, and she wouldn't stop him. He saw the longing in her eyes. The intensity matched his own need, quickly blazing out of control.

But desperate as he was to taste her lips again—lips that had consumed his thoughts for the last ten years—he couldn't do it. He couldn't kiss her. Not when he still had so much to say, to confess and amend. It wouldn't be right.

She parted her lips and released a shuddering breath. The seductive sound nearly sent him over the edge. He tensed his muscles, determined to maintain control. But if he didn't step away soon, he was in serious danger of kissing her. And with the mounting hunger coursing through his body, he couldn't trust himself to stop at one kiss.

Luckily, Cap came to his rescue.

The nutty, storm-loving dog barked again, as if to coax another wave against *Mira*'s hull. The noise broke through his single-minded concentration, and he inched back, dropping his hands at his sides. "We should try to get some sleep."

"Uh-huh," she murmured, sounding distracted. Or was it disappointment he heard?

Wishful thinking. "How's your ankle? Can you walk back?" He prayed she answered in the affirmative. He didn't want to think about what would happen if he needed to carry her.

His temperature rose as his mind conjured a vision of Sage nestled in his arms. *Get it together.*

"Good as new." She scooped her phone off the ground, flooding the galley with light. Without glancing over her shoulder, she led the way out.

For the next five minutes, while Flynn changed into dry clothes, he gave himself a pep talk.

Relax. It'll be fine. Cap will be a buffer. Just close your eyes and get some sleep. There's nothing to worry about.

He felt marginally confident in his game plan until he exited the head and caught sight of Sage snuggled in bed with Cap.

Silver light streamed through the butterfly hatch, illuminating the woman he loved as she cuddled his dog.

He was a goner.

"The waves seem to have settled," she noted, scratching Cap behind the ears. "And the rain seems softer, too."

"That's good. Maybe we'll actually get some sleep, then." *Ha! Not a chance.*

He avoided looking in her direction as he ran a hand along the bed frame. *Perfect!* Just what he'd been looking for. He flipped up the custom guardrails. "These will come in handy, just in case." He rounded the bed to her side, still averting his gaze as he locked her padded guardrail into place. Even on his best day, he couldn't handle how tempting she looked in her huggably soft pj's, with her unruly hair begging to be tangled in his fingertips.

"Thanks. That'll make me feel a lot safer. I almost spilled out of bed a dozen times."

Now, he'd be here to catch her.

He shushed his unhelpful thoughts. *Focus on sleep. Sleeeeeep.* His one-track mind seemed to struggle with the concept.

Cap wiggled, clearly in heaven, as Flynn crawled into bed on his other side.

"Did I warn you he snores?"

"That's okay." Sage nuzzled Cap's snout. "I doubt I'll be able to sleep much, anyway."

You and me both.

He plopped his head against the pillow and stared straight up at the inky black sky. Raindrops dappled the window, blurring the few stars he could see. How would his life be different if he'd gone on the sailing adventure with Sage all those years ago? He wouldn't have Cap, which was a sad thought.

Maybe he needed to focus less on rewriting the past and more on what he could do now to change the present.

Keeping his gaze fixed overhead, he asked, "What do you plan to do with *Mira* if you find the diary first?"

A long silence followed, and he almost turned to check if she was still awake. But even with Cap as a buffer, he didn't trust himself. He was too aware of her presence mere inches away.

"I want to turn her into a bookstore." When she finally spoke, her voice tiptoed across the comforter, tentative and uncertain, as if she wasn't quite sure she should trust him with her dream.

At her confession, his chest swelled with a soul-filling surge of happiness. She'd finally get her bookstore. And an even better one than he'd ever imagined.

"It's probably a silly idea," she added when he didn't respond right away.

"It's a brilliant idea. Beyond brilliant. It's unique. Creative. Special. People will come from miles away to see something like that." His excitement grew as ideas rolled in, one on top of the other. "You could even hold themed sailing charters. *Moby Dick*–inspired whale watching tours. *Treasure Island*–themed trips to the Tanti Islands off the coast of Blessings Bay."

Sage laughed softly.

"What?" he asked. "Dumb ideas?"

"No, I love them. It's like you've been thinking about this longer than I have."

He smiled in the darkness. He'd managed countless businesses over the years, but none had thrilled him as much as this one. "Tell me more about your business plan. I want to hear all the details."

Flynn wasn't sure how long they talked, but all their

brainstorming must've bored Cap because he abandoned them for the foot of the bed. Normally, Flynn would have agreed with him. Generally speaking, shop talk bored him to tears, too. But something about Sage's sailing bookshop sparked his interest in a way nothing else had before. And as he listened to all her ingenious plans, he'd never been prouder of anyone in his life. He only wished he could be a part of it.

As if the thought had just occurred to her, Sage added, "Please don't tell your mom any of this. I don't need her making things harder for me."

Flynn winced, but she had a valid point. "I'm sorry about how she's treated you. I thought after we stopped dating, she'd finally let up. Then, she opened her ridiculous bookstore. She could've opened a clothing boutique or sold snooty home decor. Anything other than books. It felt like she did it just to spite you." He'd never fully forgiven his mother for the way she'd treated Sage. Or understood why she'd been so vindictive even after they split. Squelching his rising resentment with a cleansing breath, he added, "I begged her to leave you alone and just let you be happy."

Another long silence stretched between them, punctuated by the rain and Cap's rhythmic snores.

Finally, Sage murmured, "I always suspected your mother's bookstore was a personal slight. I just didn't want to believe it." A strange laugh escaped her lips, soft and strangled by sadness. The mournful sound sliced all the way to his soul. "Honestly, I could've saved her the hassle. After losing Kevin, then you, *happy* wasn't really an option for me anymore."

Her words didn't carry any bitterness or blame. Only

raw, unfiltered heartbreak. And they hit him with all the force of a fatal blow.

For ten years, he'd lived with guilt and remorse over the way he'd ended things between them. He'd punished himself in countless ways and wouldn't let himself off the hook with excuses or rationalizations.

But he'd never done the one thing that mattered the most.

The one thing he should've done a decade ago.

He'd never apologized.

Chapter 24

SAGE

SAGE WIPED a stray tear from her eye before it dampened her pillow, thankful Flynn couldn't see her cry in the dark.

She'd imagined what it would be like to have this conversation with Flynn countless times, to finally confront him for leaving her without warning or explanation. But now that she stood on the precipice, with an open invitation to speak her mind, she couldn't find the words.

As she lay cloaked in the protective shadows of night, the *tap, tap, tap* of soothing raindrops lured her into the quiet corners of her subconscious, where she had no choice but to be self-aware.

A long-suppressed truth slipped into her thoughts. A truth her heart had always known.

She still loved Flynn Cahill.

Despite a decade of practiced denial, she couldn't lie to herself anymore.

Tonight—as they shared pieces of their lives with each other—a floodgate opened, unleashing a deluge of emotions.

But it was more than old feelings flooding to the surface. So much more.

She didn't merely love the Flynn from her past. The new Flynn, despite his misguided life choices, had captured her heart, too. With his kindness, humor, and loyalty. Loyalty that extended to his brother and Cap, but painfully, not to her.

If only she'd been good enough.

"Sage?" His hesitant voice broke through the agony of her thoughts.

"Yeah?" she whispered, not trusting herself to speak more than a syllable.

A long pause hung over them, heavy and stifling. What did he want to say?

She kneaded her bottom lip, counting each erratic heartbeat as they quickened in the expanding silence.

When Flynn finally spoke again, his words punctuated the stillness, clear and unmistakable, resonating all the way to her core. "I'm sorry."

She held her breath, as if not breathing could somehow stop time and preserve the moment. Preserve the words she'd waited ten years to hear.

"I'm so sorry," he repeated, his husky tone thick with pain. "I never should've left the way I did. I was a coward. And unforgivably selfish. I knew if I saw you and tried to explain, I wouldn't go through with it. I wouldn't be able to see you and still walk away." His voice shook as if it took considerable effort to keep his emotions at bay, and with each word he uttered, her heart broke anew.

"I never wanted to leave, but I thought I had no choice. I thought it was the right thing to do. For my parents. For Kev.

Even for you. Although, I know that doesn't make sense right now."

Tears tumbled down her cheeks, soaking her skin and the satin pillowcase. How could he possibly think he'd done her a favor by leaving her behind? It had taken her ten years to envision a future without him. And even now, with an inkling of hope for her bookstore, a future without Flynn paled in comparison to one *with* him.

"Whatever my reasons, they're not an excuse. I may have lost my brother, but you lost one of your best friends. You were hurting, too. And I left when you needed me most." His voice cracked, and so did the barricade around her heart.

All the bitterness she'd collected to coddle her tender wound slipped away, providing space to breathe—to finally heal.

"I failed you, Sage. I failed us. And that's a regret I'll carry for the rest of my life." His voice sounded closer now, as if he'd turned his head toward hers. "I don't deserve your forgiveness. But you deserve a thousand apologies. And they're all ten years overdue. I'm sorry it took me so long."

In the wake of his confession, impulse superseded thought or deliberation.

Compelled by an all-consuming need to be near him—to feel his touch—she found his hand in the darkness.

Her pulse fluttering wildly, she grazed his pinky finger with her own.

His breath hitched, and his hand wrapped around hers, tight and intense, as if he'd never let go.

They lay perfectly still, fingers entwined, cocooned by the cathartic rumble of waves and rain.

Without a word, they let their tears fall in tandem.

Tears for all they'd lost.
For all the time they'd wasted.
For everything they couldn't get back.
Each tear that fell cleared a path, making way for *maybes*.
Maybe this wasn't the end.
Maybe it was a new beginning.

SAGE

SAGE WOKE TO THE SWEET, salty scent of the ocean after the rain. Soft tendrils of sunlight streamed through the overhead window, highlighting the rumpled sheets where Flynn once slept. She caressed the faint imprint left behind on his pillow, already missing his presence.

She'd never slept more peacefully than last night, her hand clasped in Flynn's comforting grasp. She wanted to spend every night the exact same way. But how was that possible? What future could they have? Tonight at the gala, his parents would announce his promotion as the new VP of Cahill Enterprises, a position that would take him all over the country. Far, far away from Blessings Bay—away from her.

Her heart ached at the likelihood of losing him again. How would she survive a second time?

The heady fragrance of freshly brewed coffee and buttery pancakes floated into the cabin. Her stomach growled.

Oh, to marry a man who could cook like Flynn.

She shook away the foolish thought. The last thing she

needed was to dream about happily ever after when this may be their last day together.

She quickly combed her fingers through her unkempt hair before climbing out of bed. As she followed the mouth-watering aroma to the galley, her stomach swam with eagerness and apprehension. Part of her couldn't wait to see Flynn after last night—after they'd finally buried the past—but what if she'd imagined the whole thing?

Her palms warmed at the memory of his touch, tender and tingling, as if his fingerprints had left a permanent mark. *Definitely not a dream.* At the faintest brush of their pinkies, he'd reached for her, gripping tightly, as if she held all hope for a future together in her hand. It had to mean something, didn't it?

She paused in the doorway, watching the man she loved flip pancakes on the small stove, humming a happy tune. Was it "Starting Over" by John Lennon? She smiled, secretly thanking Gran for passing down her love of the Beatles.

Flynn turned off the burner and swiveled to check on the steeping French press. When he spotted her in the doorway, his smile beamed even brighter, radiating all the love she felt in her heart. Was it possible they could start over?

"Good morning." He held her gaze, and an earnest yet nervous energy crackled between them, as if neither one of them knew how to act after last night.

"Morning." She tucked a curl behind her ear, giving her fidgety fingers an outlet for their jitters.

After Flynn's apology, they hadn't spoken another word. They'd simply fallen asleep holding hands, their new status quo left unspoken.

The slate had been wiped clean, but what now?

She suddenly needed to divert attention from the strange tension in the room. "Where's Cap?"

"On deck, sunning himself. I think he's really getting used to life aboard a sailboat. He doesn't even mind doing his business on the patch of artificial turf, which I've heretofore dubbed the new poop deck."

She smiled, stopping herself from asking how he felt being on a boat again.

Flynn plunged the French press, separating the velvety liquid from the grounds. "I've been thinking a lot about your sailing bookshop."

"*Floating* bookshop," she corrected him.

"See, that's what I wanted to talk to you about. I think you can go bigger. I really think you should consider literary-themed sailing charters. And I thought of the perfect idea to convince you." He turned to face her, his amber eyes sparkling with glints of gold, the way they used to almost every day when they were younger. Back when he exuded excitement and exuberance for life. "Remember the part in *The Curious Quest of Quinley Culpepper* where Quinley saves her ship from the ruthless pirate captain by winning him over with an elaborate tea party?" He didn't wait for her to respond before blurting, "Wouldn't that make the coolest excursion? You could make it a sunset sailing tour with a pirate-themed tea party."

As he rattled off more details, Sage stood in stunned silence, certain she'd conjured the entire conversation in her mind. She had to be hallucinating.

"Sage? Did you hear anything I said?"

Sage blinked, struggling to make sense of what just transpired. "You—you read *The Curious Quest of Quinley*

Culpepper?" She'd hounded him about reading the story a hundred times as kids, but he'd always brushed it off as a "girly" book.

"Like a dozen times." He grinned. "I know, I know. As a kid, I thought it was just some book about a girl looking for her father. But once I read it, I realized it's really about the journey of finding yourself. And how the friends we make along the way help us figure it out."

He'd actually read it, after all these years. She couldn't believe it. Tears pricked her eyes. The thought of Flynn reading her favorite novel just to be close to her—and that he actually *understood* it—touched something deep in her soul, like a love language that transcended words.

Without thinking, she spanned the distance between them and flung her arms around his neck. Their lips met with a spark of electricity she'd never felt before, urgent, fierce, and utterly sublime.

Flynn pulled her close, one hand encircling her waist while the other cradled the nape of her neck, deepening the kiss. His fingertips flexed, deliciously tangled in her curls, as if they'd ached to caress them again.

She lost herself in the moment, blissfully aware of each thrilling sensation, from the top of her head to her toes.

Oh, how she'd missed this. She'd missed *him*. And right now, nothing else mattered. Not even the heartbreak that would inevitably follow.

When their lips finally parted, Flynn rested his forehead against hers as he caught his breath. "Wow," he murmured with the sultriest rasp. "I guess you liked my idea."

She laughed softly, savoring his scent. "I loved it. But setting aside the fact that we still haven't found the diary, so I don't yet have a boat to sail, I can't exactly afford to hire a crew."

"What about me?"

At his unexpected question, she stepped back to search his gaze. "What are you saying?"

"What if I sail *Mira* for you?" His eyes gleamed again.

"You?" He couldn't be serious.

"Sure, I'm a little rusty. But I bet it'll all come back to me in no time. Plus"—his lips arched in an impish smirk—"we make a pretty good team, don't you think?"

She blushed. Her lips still tingled from his kiss. "But what about your promotion? You can't run Cahill Enterprises *and* a sailing charter."

"True. But Kev's list is thirty before *thirty*. I still have time before I hit the big 3-0." He grinned proudly, as if he'd thought of everything.

Her pulse fluttered at the possibility. Could this actually work?

But what happens next year? And the year after that?

Sage shoved her concerns to the back of her subconscious. Tomorrow's problems could take care of themselves. "Your parents aren't going to be happy."

"I know." For the first time that morning, the light in his eyes dimmed. "And I feel bad about letting them down. But I've spent my entire life trying to please them. For once, I want to do something for us."

For us. The words wrapped around her like a warm embrace. "Are you sure?"

"So sure, why don't we skip the coffee and go straight for the champagne to celebrate?" He grabbed a bottle of Dom Pérignon from the fridge.

She couldn't help a smile. "I guess Mr. Mackensie's provisions weren't so impractical after all."

"I'm starting to wonder if he knew something we didn't." Flynn tossed her another teasing grin and twisted the cork.

With a loud pop and a whoosh, the cork sailed into the air and thwacked against the fancy crown molding that framed the ceiling.

Giddy with mounting happiness, Sage laughed, then gasped as a six-inch section of the crown molding swung open, revealing a narrow crevice.

"That's weird." Flynn frowned.

"You don't think—" *No. It couldn't be.*

Flynn hoisted himself onto the counter. "What are the chances we just found Mira's secret stash?"

"A hundred to one?" Her heart raced, but she didn't dare hope.

Flynn stuck his hand into the shadowy nook. His eyes widened. Both disbelief and triumph splashed across his face as he withdrew his hand. Along with a small leather-bound notebook.

Her pulse slowed to a standstill. "Is it—?"

Flynn flipped it open, briefly glanced at the first page, then met her gaze with the biggest, goofiest grin. "I think we've won ourselves a sailboat."

Happy tears welled, creating a surreal, dreamlike effect as Flynn whooped and scooped her off the ground, twirling her around the tiny room.

Cap clearly heard all the commotion from above deck because he barreled through the companionway to join the celebration, barking and prancing along with them.

The entire scene played out in slow motion, and Sage tried to memorize each exquisite detail, down to the fizzy champagne bubbles that tickled her throat.

But somewhere deep in her heart, a quiet voice wondered, *Was it all a little too good to be true?*

Chapter 26

ABBY

ABBY SET the vintage glass vase in the precise center of the small patio table, then turned it clockwise so the largest ivory tea rose unfolded its velveteen petals toward the balcony doors. Every detail needed to be perfect for when Sadie Hamilton and her friend Lucy arrived that afternoon.

She shifted the matching chairs half an inch to maximize the view of the Pacific Ocean and verdant garden below. She imagined the two women savoring their morning coffee while golden streaks of sunlight glittered across the water.

There really wasn't a more beautiful spot in all the world.

During one final inspection of the balcony, Abby swiped her finger along the glossy white railing. *Huh.* Not a single speck of dust. She hadn't expected Piper to be so thorough. In fact, after a day and a half of working together, Piper had surpassed her expectations in every way. She'd not only performed each task Abby assigned with the utmost professionalism, she often went above and beyond the initial request, like watching video tutorials detailing how to fold hand towels into the shape of a rosebud. *Ugh.* Why couldn't

Piper skate by on the bare minimum so she'd have another reason to dislike her?

Guilt knotted in the pit of her stomach. She'd never experienced such complicated emotions toward another living being. Under other circumstances, she might even like Piper. But how could you like a woman claiming to be your husband's one-night stand?

Anxiety rose in her chest, and Abby pressed a hand to her collarbone to suppress the nervous fluttering. Lately, she'd subsisted on stress and sips of coffee, which only added to her already soaring cortisol levels. Thankfully, the nightmarish ordeal would be over soon.

The test results would arrive any day now. She'd asked a friend at the post office to be on the lookout and special deliver them as soon as possible. But the thought of finally holding the results in her own two hands wasn't completely devoid of trepidation. Although she knew Donnie had loved her more than anything, could a woman ever truly be certain of her husband's fidelity?

The lingering question made her queasy, and she tried to dispel the unpleasant thought with positive affirmations. *Don't let her get to you. You trusted Donnie. He loved you. He would never hurt you.*

Breathing a little easier, she performed one last sweep of the suite and headed downstairs.

The sweet, spicy scent of cinnamon and sugar wafted down the hall, and her pulse spiked. She did a quick mental tally. Logan was on an errand in town. Max and Tyler were at Verna's. That left only one other person in the house.

A sickening dread coated the back of her throat, and she struggled to swallow.

Please, anyone but her.

With her eyes closed, Abby pushed open the kitchen door. The telltale aroma of fresh-from-the-oven snickerdoodles assaulted her senses. Her stomach turned, and she slowly opened her eyes.

Piper stood in *her* kitchen—her sacred space—wearing *her* apron and oven mitts. Warm, golden mounds of melt-in-your-mouth goodness cooled on wire racks, and baking supplies littered the countertops. Piper hummed along to some pop song playing on her phone. She was disheveled and speckled with flour, but that wasn't what struck Abby the most.

For the first time since she arrived, Piper was smiling.

Abby stared, unable to move, as simmering resentment bubbled to the surface.

Oblivious to her audience, Piper slid another tray into the oven. Swaying her hips to the music, she plucked a piece of dough from the mixing bowl and popped it into her mouth. She looked so comfortable, so at ease. As if the space Abby had lovingly made her own over the last year and a half belonged to her.

"Wh-what are you doing?" Abby's voice quivered.

Piper jumped, then relaxed when she spotted Abby. "Sorry, I didn't see you come in." She pressed Pause on her playlist. "Don't worry. I'll clean up the mess."

"What do you think you're doing?" Abby repeated, startled by the tremor of adrenaline and apprehension vibrating in her chest.

"I—" Piper hesitated when she caught Abby's stricken expression. "I—I read about a boutique hotel that offered their guests freshly baked cookies at check-in. I can't cook to save my life, but I can bake a killer snickerdoodle. I—I thought you might like to offer your guests one."

"You have no right to be in here." To Abby's horror, hot tears pooled in her eyes, as if all the emotions she'd been fighting to control over the last few days suddenly needed somewhere to go.

"I—I'm sorry." Piper blinked in surprise. "I didn't mean to upset you. I didn't think—"

"That's the problem," Abby interrupted, tears spilling down her cheeks, no matter how desperately she tried to stop them. "You didn't *think*. You just did what you wanted, regardless of how it affects other people." Abby furiously scrubbed her damp face with the heel of her hand, mortified by her outburst. What was wrong with her?

Piper's features softened as if she understood Abby's reaction better than she did, as if she knew it had very little to do with the kitchen and everything to do with Donnie. She gingerly removed the apron and folded it on the counter. "You're right. I should've asked first. I'm really sorry, Abby."

Abby stopped short at the sincerity in Piper's voice. Had she just apologized? Her dismay slowly subsided, making room for rational thought. "It's okay." She inhaled a shaky breath, suddenly overcome with emotional exhaustion and a strange, almost cathartic sense of release. "I'm the one who should apologize. I overreacted. You were just trying to be helpful." She glanced at the bakery-worthy snickerdoodles cooling on the kitchen island—the evidence of Piper's hard work and kind intentions. "The cookies are a good idea."

"Thanks. They taste even better than they look." Piper smiled as she offered her one.

Abby accepted the perfectly plump peace offering, but

before she could take a bite, a throat cleared behind them. She turned, the snickerdoodle poised halfway to her mouth.

Tina, her tattooed aerobics instructor friend at the post office, hovered in the doorway, glancing warily between them.

Abby's gaze fell to the envelope in her hand.

Her heart stopped, and she stole a glance at Piper.

An odd, unreadable glint sparked in the other woman's eyes.

Panic? Dread? Misgiving?

One thing was certain.

They both knew exactly what Tina held in her hands.

Chapter 27

ABBY

THE ENVELOPE WEIGHED HEAVILY in Abby's hands as she thanked Tina for the special delivery. Her friend scurried out of the kitchen as if she couldn't escape the awkward tension fast enough. Although, Abby suspected within minutes the entire town would be crowded outside with their ears pressed to the door, waiting for the final word on her husband's alleged affair.

In Tina's absence, an oppressive silence permeated the room, punctuated by the repetitive *tick, tick, tick* of the wall clock.

Piper stood stock-still, eyes wide like a deer facing down its inevitable doom in the bright lights of oncoming traffic. Her entire ruse would unravel in a matter of seconds.

And Abby would finally be free from the torment of uncertainty.

She slid one finger into the corner of the envelope seal, then hesitated. Maybe she should wait for Logan? He'd been by her side every step of the way. He wouldn't want to miss this moment. But how long until he returned? She had no idea.

Stop stalling, Abby.

She gritted her teeth, stilling her jaw's anxious twitching.

You have nothing to worry about. Get it over with already.

She inserted her finger deeper into the seal, prepared to rip it open.

"Wait!" Piper stepped toward her, both palms extended. "Don't open it."

"Why not? This is what we've been waiting for. It's the whole reason you're here, isn't it?" Tears of frustration burned in her eyes again. When would this woman stop playing games?

"I know. It's just—" Piper's features crumpled. Abby had never seen someone look so defeated, so painfully helpless.

"What? What aren't you telling me?"

Piper glanced up at the ceiling, fighting off the onset of her own tears. Finally, she met Abby's gaze, visibly broken. "Because I lied, okay?" She stifled a sob, her lips quivering. "I lied about having an affair with Donnie. He's not Tyler's father."

Piper's words crashed over her, offering relief, except she found no comfort in her confession. No vindication. No reprieve.

Instead, she felt a crushing numbness.

"I'm sorry." Piper turned off the oven without checking on the cookies inside. With a crazed, manic energy, she tidied her mess, shoving dirty dishes into the sink, swiping crumbs into piles. "You've been nothing but nice to me since we got here. You took us in. You gave me a job. You didn't have to do that. Most women wouldn't." Piper shook her head as if she still couldn't believe it. "You've treated me with kindness. And I've done nothing but hurt you." She froze midfrenzy, as if the weight of her actions finally hit her full force. "I never should've come here. I never should've let it get this far." She turned, fixing her gaze on the envelope in Abby's hand. "I have to make it right."

Before Abby could stop her, Piper yanked the envelope from her grasp. "What are you doing?" Abby cried.

"What I should've done days ago. I'm going to pack our things, pick up Tyler from Verna's, and get out of your life for good." Piper made a beeline for the door, colliding with Logan on his way into the kitchen.

"Whoa!" Logan stepped aside as Piper barreled past him. "What's up with her? Was she crying?"

Abby couldn't speak, too stunned by Piper's reaction to form a coherent sentence.

"Are you okay? What happened?" Logan verbalized her thoughts as he rushed to her side.

"I—I don't know." She struggled to piece together the chain of events. "Tina delivered the test results—"

"Hallelujah! If they didn't arrive soon, I was this close to going to the lab myself." Grinning, he pinched his fingers together, leaving a centimeter of space. When she didn't return his smile, he squinted in confusion. "Is that why Piper ran out of here so upset? Because her little scheme finally blew up in her face when you read the results?"

"That's the weird thing," Abby said slowly, still in a daze. "I didn't even get a chance. She confessed to making up the whole thing. She went upstairs to pack."

"Huh." Logan frowned, then shrugged. "Well, I guess

she saved you the trouble. At any rate, she's finally out of our hair."

For some reason, Abby couldn't bring herself to share his enthusiasm. Something about the whole bizarre exchange didn't sit quite right with her.

He picked up on her reservation. "Don't worry, Abs. I'll check in with Piper before she leaves. I'll make sure the money she made working here is enough to get her back on her feet. We won't send Tyler back on the road without a game plan, okay?"

Nodding, she attempted a smile.

She should be happy the nightmare had finally ended.

And yet, she couldn't shake the uncomfortable feeling that there was something else going on.

Something she'd missed.

LOGAN

LOGAN WATCHED Abby move around the kitchen tidying up the mess in dazed, mechanical movements, her brow knit with worry. Why wasn't she happier that Piper finally came clean?

He was about to ask her when there was a knock at the door.

Abby's eyes widened, increasing from worry to full-on panic mode. "That must be Sadie and Lucy. They're early." She froze, a damp dish towel hovering over a glop of cookie dough on the counter as if she didn't know what to do next.

"Hey." He crossed the kitchen and placed both hands on her shoulders, peering deep into her eyes. "Everything's going to be great. You've got this."

Her features relaxed as he drew her into his arms for a quick, reassuring hug. "You're right," she sighed. "I just need to put Piper out of my mind for the moment." She straightened and slid two warm cookies onto a plate. "I can do this. Welcoming guests to Blessings on State Street is one of the best parts of the job."

"That's the spirit." He flashed a grin, adding, "I'll come with you and help carry their luggage," and followed a few steps behind for moral support.

But when Abby opened the door, they didn't find Sadie and Lucy standing on the front porch.

Instead, Donnie's lawyer, Victor Fuentes, skulked in the shadows like a neighborhood kid about to apologize for hitting a foul ball through their window.

Logan had met the guy only once, almost six years ago when he'd accepted the job as caretaker of Donnie's beach house in Blessings Bay. Victor, not Donnie, had been the one to meet him at the house, go over the paperwork, and give him a rundown of his responsibilities.

And over the last six years, Victor had been his go-to guy, the one to cut his checks and answer any questions he had about the property and his duties. Through all their dealings, he'd seemed like a no-nonsense, genuine guy. Not cocky, but confident. Nothing like the sheepish man currently avoiding his gaze.

"Victor. Hi." Abby couldn't hide her surprise but still managed a welcoming smile. "It's so nice to see you. Please, come in." She stepped aside, and Victor shuffled inside. "What brings you all this way?"

"I have the financial documents you requested." He pulled a thick manila envelope from his briefcase, but Logan wasn't buying it. He could've sent the information Abby needed electronically or by registered mail. There had to be another reason for his impromptu visit. A reason he probably wouldn't like.

Logan stood by Abby's side, waiting for the other shoe to

drop. And from the way Victor kept shifting his feet, the sole would be worn clear through to the floor.

"Thank you. But personal delivery really wasn't necessary." She tucked the envelope under her arm, then held out the plate. "Cookie? They're snickerdoodles, straight from the oven."

"Uh, no. No, thank you." Was Victor sweating?

Whatever it is, just spill the beans already, Logan silently urged.

Victor swallowed, and his Adam's apple protruded as if he'd gulped down a golf ball. *Yeesh*. The guy was a wreck.

"Th-there's actually another reason I'm here." He tugged on his collar. "It's rather embarrassing."

"What is it?" Abby's voice rose warily.

"I've been practicing law for over twenty-five years, and nothing like this has ever happened." Victor glanced between them, then down at the floor.

"Victor, what's wrong?" Abby pressed. "You're making me nervous."

Victor exhaled, and his shoulders slumped in the telltale posture of a man resigned to his unfortunate fate. "When I was going through your file, I discovered I'd made a terrible oversight." The tips of his ears turned pink as he pulled another envelope from his briefcase. This time, a small white one. "I found a letter from Mr. Preston. A letter he wrote nearly six years ago. And that I was supposed to deliver upon his death."

"Oh." The color drained from Abby's cheeks, and she took a moment to process the information.

Logan placed a hand on the small of her back with the instinctive need to steady her, both physically and emotionally. A letter from Donnie from beyond the grave? That was some heavy stuff. He couldn't imagine how she felt right now.

After a long pause, Abby held out her hand for the envelope, but Victor shook his head. "My apologies. I should have been clearer." He turned toward Logan. "The letter is for Mr. Mathews."

"Me?" Logan balked. "Are you sure?"

"Quite sure. And please accept my sincerest apologies for the delayed delivery." He handed Logan the envelope then bid them an awkward, mumbled goodbye before letting himself out.

Logan held the letter in his hands, too flummoxed to speak. Why had Donnie left him a letter? Was it about the house? The timeline matched, since according to Victor, he'd written it shortly after he'd inherited the place.

He had expected to hear something after Donnie's death, but when he hadn't, he'd simply carried on as usual, taking care of the house the same way he always had. He'd continued to receive checks from Victor, so why upset the status quo?

He cleared his throat. "I guess we should read it, huh?" He glanced at Abby. Was it weird to read a letter from her ex-husband—one of his best friends—now that they were together? How would Donnie feel about him dating and hopefully *marrying* the woman he loved?

He'd asked himself that question a hundred times and always landed on the same answer. Donnie would want Abby to be looked after, to be cherished. He'd be happy for them.

But what if, by some freakish turn of events, this letter said otherwise? What if Donnie asked him to stay away from

Abby? Would he honor his friend's request? Or worse—would Abby want him to?

Uncertainty swirled in his stomach, but he pressed on anyway, tearing open the seal. "Should we read it together?"

She kneaded her lips, then shook her head. "No. I don't think so. It's addressed to you. You should read it first."

"You sure?"

"I'm sure. I'll take these back to the kitchen." She lifted the plate of cookies and forced a smile, but it didn't fool him. She looked as rattled by what could be in Donnie's letter as he felt.

He waited until she disappeared down the hall before sliding out the single sheet of notebook paper.

His heart pounded at Donnie's chicken scratch hand-writing covering the page.

Nugget,

A flutter of warmth filled his chest at the familiarity in the greeting. Of course Donnie would address the letter with his call sign—the call sign Donnie had made stick thanks to the care packages Logan's grandmother sent him loaded with his favorite dessert, Nevada Nuggets. He'd hated the name at first, but once his grandmother passed away, he'd viewed it as a tribute. Funny how losing someone can change your perspective so profoundly.

If you're reading this, I finally kicked the bucket. Which shocks me as much as it does you. Remember when we thought we'd live forever?

His heart twisted as Donnie's voice filled the room. He could hear his bright, boisterous baritone so clearly.

Well played, Death. You finally got your man. We had a good run.

Logan could picture Donnie's jovial grin. He never seemed to take things too seriously. Even death.

Here's the thing, Nugget. I'm not afraid of dying. I'm afraid of what will happen after I'm gone. To the people I love. To one person above all.

Logan's pulse spiked, and apprehension skated up his spine. He had to mean Abby. But what was he so afraid of?

You haven't met Abby yet, but you will soon. Man, how I envy you. Meeting Abby for the first time was the best moment of my life. I'll try to put it in words you'll understand. Remember the first time you flew the A-4 Skyhawk? You said it was like strapping a rocket to your back. Well, buddy, meeting Abby is kinda like that. Only a million times better.

Logan couldn't help a small smile at the analogy. Donnie's description was spot-on.

I know you think I did you some kind of favor when I hired you to manage the house in Blessings Bay. And as good as my legs look in superhero tights, it's time I set the record straight. Honestly, I should've done it a long time ago.

A heavy weight of foreboding settled on Logan's shoulders. What was Donnie about to confess?

The truth is, I'm no hero. Far from it. In fact, you're the one doing me a favor. You see, I need to keep the house for Abby. I know she'll love it. One day, she'll probably want to make it her home. But not now. Not when there's a chance she'll discover my secret.

The last word leaped off the page, and Logan felt sick to his stomach.

This couldn't be happening. He refused to believe his friend had an affair. And yet, Donnie had written the words with his own hand. *My secret.* Was it possible he meant something besides an affair?

Man, Nugget, this is hard to admit. Especially to you. You always saw the best in me. You kept me on the straight and narrow like my own personal Jiminy Cricket in a G suit. I hate to let you down.

Logan looked away. His eyes suddenly felt hot and itchy. *Come on, Donnie. Tell me you didn't do it.* He rubbed his eyes with his knuckles and forced himself to look back at the letter.

Even worse than letting you down, I let Abby down. She trusted me, and I betrayed that trust. It was only the one time, and I never contacted the woman again, but it doesn't change facts. I screwed up. I did the unforgivable. And no matter how hard I try to make up for it, I know I can't.

A guttural groan rose in Logan's throat like a lament from deep within his soul. His heart ached for Abby's sake. How could Donnie do this to her? And how was he going to tell her?

A spark of anger flared in his chest. Donnie cheated on Abby and proposed anyway—without telling her the truth. And then the coward waited until he died and made him do the dirty work.

Logan resisted the overwhelming urge to crumple the letter and toss it in the trash. There wasn't anything Donnie could say to assuage the ball of fury blazing through his veins.

You probably hate me right now. And I don't blame you. I kinda hate myself. I've tried to bury the guilt, determined to be a better man. The kind of man Abby deserves. Although, I know I don't even come close. But I hope and pray she knows

180

how much I love her. That what I did had every-
thing to do with my own fears and insecurities and
nothing to do with her not being good enough.
Man, Nugget. Even writing those words—knowing
how much I hurt her—kills me. It kills me that I
could be so selfish. So stupid. And Abby's going to
pay the price.

Logan's jaw flexed with another flash of anger.
Donnie had no idea how hefty a price.

I've thought about telling her the truth. I've
come close a few times. But I'm a coward. I can't
handle the thought of losing her. She's the best
thing in my life. Once you meet her, you'll
understand.

Oh, he understood. He also knew that loving someone
meant putting their best interest above your own. And
Donnie had dropped the ball. Big-time.

If Abby moves to Blessings Bay like I think
she will, the truth will eventually come out. It's the
kind of small town where everyone knows every-
thing about everyone. Think Mayberry by the
beach. The woman I mentioned works at one of the
only restaurants in town. They're bound to meet.
Maybe even become friends. I can't stomach the

RACHAEL BLOOME

thought of Abby being blindsided without someone there to support her, to help her through it.

Which leads me to my big request. I know it's asking a lot. And you can curse me under your breath all you want. But I need you to tell Abby the truth, so it comes from someone I trust.

And then I'm gonna need one final favor. Not because I deserve it. Or because you owe me anything. Do it for Abby.

Take care of her, Logan. She's a heck of a lot stronger and braver than she realizes, but I don't want her to go through this alone.

She's going to need someone like you. Someone steady and trustworthy. Someone loyal. Someone better than I ever was.

And please, tell her that I love her.

And that I'm sorry.

The raw humility in Donnie's words—and the way he used his given name this time—broke something in Logan's heart. His defenses crumbled. His anger softened. And the dull ache grew more intense.

He missed Donnie. Sure, if he saw him right now, he'd slug him good and hard before he hugged him. But he still wanted to hug his stupid, selfish, spineless friend. He couldn't explain it. Despite all the awful things he'd done, he wanted Donnie to make amends with Abby and meet his son.

Over the last few months, he'd had a taste of fatherhood,

thanks to Max. He loved that kid as if he'd known him his whole life, as if he were his own. He wished Donnie could have that same gift. To experience firsthand how the love of a child can make you a better man.

But it was too late.

Donnie's lie had cost him more than he'd ever know.

His gaze fell to the last few lines, cinching the knot around his heart even tighter.

> *There are no goodbyes. Only see you laters.*
> *So, see you later, old man.*
> *Donnie*

Tears blurred the final sendoff, but Logan didn't care.

He didn't bother hiding them or wiping them away.

He let them fall, both for the pain from the past and the pain yet to come.

The pain in which he would now play a part.

When he gave Abby the letter to read for herself.

Chapter 29

ABBY

ABBY'S KNEES BUCKLED. She sank onto the sofa, the letter shaking in her hands. A tear slid down her cheek, dampening the page. The long-dried ink bled, muddling the words *I'm sorry* into an indiscernible mess.

Just as well. How could she forgive Donnie for what he'd done?

From the moment Piper first arrived, she'd wrestled with the possibility of her worst fears becoming reality. She'd grieved a hundred times over already, combatting every doubt until she felt nothing but empty exhaustion.

And yet, the tangible proof—hearing the crushing confession in Donnie's own voice as if he stood in the room with her—filled her body with a white-hot heat of anguish that penetrated all the way to her bones.

This time, she couldn't soothe her wounds with the fragile safety of uncertainty. Her only choice was to face the truth, and somehow find a path forward. A path that completely eluded her.

The sofa cushion shifted as Logan sat beside her. "I'm so

sorry, Abs." His raspy voice strained with shared sadness. He reached for her hand, but he didn't press her to talk about her feelings or insist that everything would be okay. He merely sat with her, filling the space with his strong, steady presence, absorbing some of her sorrow.

At least Donnie had done one thing right. She couldn't imagine going through this without Logan. Could Donnie have guessed how close they'd become?

The sound of luggage wheels rolling across the hardwood floor snapped Abby from her thoughts.

Piper stood in the doorway, assessing Abby's tears with wide, worry-filled eyes. "What happened?"

Abby flinched. The sight of Piper—the woman who'd spent a night with the man she'd loved and trusted with her whole heart—felt like a stinging slap.

Logan's grip tightened. "We know." His tone rumbled across the room like a low growl.

"How?" Piper breathed, as if she knew exactly what he meant.

"Donnie confessed in a letter he wrote shortly after your affair. His lawyer was supposed to deliver it after Donnie died and just now discovered his mistake," Logan explained, mercifully speaking so she didn't have to. "But I still don't get it, Piper. Why come forward now? After all these years. And then why lie about the paternity test results? They would've proven your story. Isn't that what you wanted?"

A long, agonizing silence followed Logan's question. Abby focused on a spot on the floor, her hands trembling as she fought an overwhelming urge to flee to somewhere she could pretend like none of this had ever happened.

"Can I speak to Abby?" Piper asked softly. "Alone?"

"I don't think that's a good idea." Logan sat rooted to the sofa, steadfast and immovable. Her rock. Somehow, even in the midst of devastation, her heart had room to mourn one love while bursting with immeasurable affection and appreciation for another.

"It's okay." Spurred by his unfailing support, she found the strength to squeeze his hand. "I think I need to hear what she has to say."

"Are you sure?"

"I think so."

"Want me to stay? I can stay."

"I'll be okay." She couldn't be certain of that fact, but she had a feeling Piper would hold back with Logan in the room. And she needed to hear everything the woman had to say, no matter how painful.

"Okay. If you're sure. But I'll be two feet away in the kitchen when you need me."

When you need me.

Her heart warmed at his words. It wasn't a question. No *if* or *maybe.* They were a team, together through it all. Even this. And she would forever be grateful.

As Logan strode from the room—tossing a warning glance at Piper as he left—Abby girded herself with Logan's promise. He would always be here for her.

Leaving her luggage, Piper crept closer, her steps cautious and tentative, as if Abby might pounce like a wounded animal.

Piper's pretty features contorted with guilt and grief, a hunter showing remorse to its prey. She perched on the edge of the coffee table, her shoulders slumped. "I'm so sorry I hurt you."

She offered no excuses. No fancy, flowery words. Just a simple, sincere apology.

Abby forced herself to meet Piper's gaze. The woman's piercing green eyes shimmered with unshed tears. Abby gathered a breath, then exhaled slowly before asking the one question Donnie couldn't. "Why didn't you tell Donnie about Tyler?"

Piper's gaze flickered toward the floor, then back to Abby, her features firmly set as if she'd resolved to tell the whole truth, no matter what. "Because Donnie made it perfectly clear he didn't want kids. And if he didn't want children with the woman he loved and planned to marry, how would he feel about having one with me, his biggest regret?"

There was a raw, pained vulnerability in Piper's eyes that stirred unwelcome sympathy in Abby's heart. She wanted to dislike Piper, pure and simple. It wasn't right that she'd slept with Donnie. And it wasn't fair that she'd beaten the odds and had a child with him when she couldn't. And yet, despite everything, compassion complicated Abby's emotions more than she cared to admit, even to herself.

"As soon as I realized I was pregnant, I moved down south and started over. I got a new apartment, a new job. A new life. For me and Tyler."

"Then why come forward now?"

"I wish I hadn't." Piper picked at a loose thread on her ripped jeans. "I never wanted anything from Donnie. Or you. But I—" She broke away, wincing as she struggled to finish her admission. "I was desperate," she said at last, shrinking even smaller as she leaned forward, wringing her hands. "I lost my job and was close to losing my apartment. My landlord said he'd discount my rent if I did him a favor." A crimson blush swept across Piper's face, and Abby shuddered, afraid for what that favor might have entailed.

"He said all I had to do was let him have a few packages delivered to my door every couple of weeks. I'd let him know when they arrived, and he'd come pick them up. It worked out fine for a while."

"And you never wondered what might be in those packages?" Abby asked. She'd watched enough crime TV to make an educated guess. More than likely, Piper had agreed to be a drug drop-off.

"I didn't want to wonder. I didn't want to know. I just wanted to keep me and Tyler from living on the streets."

"So, what happened?" Clearly, something had gone awry, or they wouldn't be living out of their car.

"One of the packages went missing, and my landlord accused me of taking it. I swore I never touched it, but he said I had to pay him back or he'd..." Piper's voice fell away, but she didn't have to finish her sentence. Based on her terrified expression, Abby suspected he'd threatened Tyler. Or maybe both of them.

Her stomach turned at the thought. "How much do you owe him?"

Piper looked away again, biting her lower lip. "Six thousand dollars."

Abby's heart sank. "Six thousand?" she echoed in a whisper.

Piper nodded, suddenly pale. "I don't have that kind of money. Or *any* money. So, I packed up our things and ran. But he hasn't stopped calling, demanding his money. He said no matter where I go, or even if I change my number, he'll know how to find us." Piper shuddered. "My only option was to get the money somehow. Desperate, I Googled Donnie. That's when I learned he'd passed away. I'm so sorry for your loss."

The rote sentiment sounded strange coming from Piper, the mother of her husband's son. How did Piper feel about Donnie's death? Had she cared for him at all? And what about Tyler? He'd never know his father now.

The thought roused fresh tears to her eyes, and her throat tightened. Donnie may not have wanted kids initially, but he would've loved Tyler. And he would've been a wonderful father, despite his flaws.

"After I found out about Donnie, I looked up what happened to the house," Piper told her. "I found an article on you and the inn, how well it was doing." She cringed as if ashamed of her own admission. "I didn't think. I just got in the car and drove. I'm so sorry, Abby. For everything."

For a long moment, Abby didn't respond. A thousand thoughts and emotions tumbled in her mind. She tried to make sense of them, to connect them together like puzzle pieces. But nothing seemed to fit. "Why didn't you tell the police?"

"Tell them what? That I unwittingly agreed to be a drug drop-off location, and the dealer thinks I stole his stash?"

She had a point. Piper had made a string of appallingly bad decisions. Horrifying, actually. She didn't deserve her pity or compassion.

And yet, as Abby looked at the woman sitting across from her, she saw someone scared, broken, and helpless. A mother who loved her son—Donnie's son—and didn't know how to untangle the mess she'd made.

An image of Tyler's sweet face flashed in the forefront of her thoughts. None of this was his fault. And yet, he would pay the price for all their decisions. *Even hers.*

Could she let them walk away without a second thought?

A gentle knock at the door made Abby jump.

She glanced at the grandfather clock.

Based on the time, it had to be Sadie and Lucy.

Strange how life didn't stop even after your whole world fell apart.

SAGE

"Do you think this is a mistake?" Sage met CeCe's gaze in the reflection of the full-length mirror in her bedroom. Her best friend sat cross-legged on the edge of the twin bed, hugging Sage's favorite throw pillow—a tufted circle with tiny honeybees embroidered by Gran—as she offered running commentary on the various outfits.

CeCe tilted her head to one side, assessing the coral cocktail dress Sage held just beneath her chin. She scrunched her nose. "Orange isn't your best color."

"I don't mean the dress." Sage sighed and shoved the hanger back into her closet.

"You mean the gala?" CeCe asked.

"The gala. The sailing-charter bookstore. Flynn. All of it." She placed both hands on the back of her head like a runner with a side cramp, trying to calm her racing heartbeat.

From the moment they found the diary earlier that morning, everything happened so quickly. Flynn contacted Herman with the good news, then ran off to tell his parents his decision to postpone the promotion. Which they would undoubtedly perceive as extremely *bad* news.

Sage shivered in her satin slip. If Cordelia hadn't loathed her before, this would clinch the deal, for sure.

She envisioned the pinched scowl on Cordelia's face when she arrived at the gala as Flynn's plus-one. Cordelia wouldn't make a scene, but she would be seething beneath the surface. And would most likely make Sage pay in some way later on.

At least she had Flynn by her side this time.

"If you're asking whether or not I think it's a mistake to forgive the love of your life for a youthful transgression and let yourself be happy for once, then no, I don't think it's a mistake," CeCe said with an air of confidence Sage wished she felt.

Was it really that simple?

Her thoughts swirling, Sage stared blankly at her closet. The collection of vintage and bohemian-inspired clothing blended together in an indiscernible kaleidoscope of colors and patterns. She'd never struggled to pick an outfit before. Why couldn't she make a decision?

"Here." CeCe hopped off the bed and shuffled through the hangers before retrieving a long, elegant gown of the palest green lace. The sweet flutter sleeves offset the more daring, figure-hugging silhouette. "This will look incredible on you. The sage color matches your eyes. And your name." CeCe smirked.

"You don't think it's a bit too va-va-voom?" She fingered the tiny silver beads dotting the fabric. She'd borrowed the dress from her mother's closet for some event she couldn't remember but hadn't wound up wearing it after all.

"Don't worry, Cinderella. It'll be perfect for a gala at the Cahill castle." CeCe's dark eyes held a playful glint.

"Does this make you my fairy godmother, then?"

"More like Q," CeCe teased, referencing an omnipotent *Star Trek* character with the power to grant your every whim. "Your wish is my command."

"Speaking of wishes, I *wish* I didn't know what you're talking about," Sage said with a laugh. "I just hope someday you find a guy as nerdy as you." She bit her tongue, immediately regretting her comment. It would take more than a fellow *Star Trek* fanatic for CeCe to forget her lifelong crush on small-town hunk turned Hollywood heartthrob, Jayce Hunt.

"Before we spend too much energy discussing things that will never happen, let's focus on how you're *not* going to blow it with Flynn by second-guessing yourself." CeCe's features softened. "It really sounds like things will be different this time."

"I hope so." Sage slid the dress over her head, then waited for CeCe to zip up the back before turning to face the mirror.

Her heartbeat stuttered. Was that *her*?

The dress fit like a dream, molding to every curve as if she'd been dipped in liquid aventurine—her favorite sage-green gemstone.

"Wow," CeCe breathed. "Maybe I missed my calling as a personal stylist. You look amazing."

"It is flattering, isn't it?" Sage swished from side to side, mesmerized by the sparkling sheen. She'd never looked so elegant. Even Cordelia would approve.

Would Flynn like it? Her cheeks heated at the thought.

"Who wants to try some black tea with honey, ginger, and turmeric? I need a few guinea pigs for my new recipe." Her mother stopped in the doorway with a tray of iced tea and two glasses. "Oh, honeybee." She gasped when she spotted her daughter wearing her dress. "You look stunning."

"Thanks." Sage warmed at her mother's compliment. "It's okay if I wear it to the gala?"

"Of course! I'm happy it's getting some use. It's always been my favorite."

"I'm surprised. You don't usually like anything this fancy." Her mother's idea of formal wear consisted of wearing a bra with underwire. Normally, she lived in loose cotton dresses and linen palazzo pants.

Her mother's eyes glazed over with a nostalgic glimmer. "Your father bought me that dress for a company Christmas party. It was held on a yacht. I'll never forget that night."

"Oh! I didn't realize. I'll find something else to wear." Sage yanked the sleeve down over her shoulder, prepared to wriggle out of the offending gown.

Why hadn't her mother tossed it after her father left?

"Don't be silly." Her mom set the tray on the dresser and moved to stand beside her. She lifted the sleeve and draped it back over her shoulder, fussing with the ruffle. "It looks perfect on you. And I know I don't talk about your father very often, but I still cherish many of our memories. It wasn't all bad, you know." Her mother met her gaze in the mirror and smiled.

Sage's heart squeezed. She did know. She had her own smattering of special memories from before her father left. At least, memories that would be special, if he'd decided to stick around.

The way her dad would push her across the carpet in a cardboard box, and she'd pretend to be a pirate queen or an astronaut. Or all the times they'd bring snacks to the airport and watch the planes take off, imagining the magical places they'd explore above the clouds.

They'd been happy once.

And then he'd disappeared as if he'd never existed at all.

"Do you think he ever regrets leaving us?" she whispered, voicing the question she'd carried in her heart for years.

"Oh, I know he does," her mother said so matter-of-factly Sage jerked her head up in surprise.

"How do you know?"

"Because he called me six months ago and said he'd made a mistake marrying Susan. He wanted to know if I'd give him a second chance."

"What did you say?" Her heart slowed to the faintest flutter.

"I told him the truth. That he doesn't really want me back. He just doesn't want to stay in a relationship when things get hard. So, he blames the other person. He blames the marriage. He makes every excuse to give himself an easy way out."

"So, you told him no?" Sage wasn't sure if she felt proud or disappointed.

"I told him he'd always be your father, should he ever realize it's the greatest role of his life. But he gave up the right to be my husband the day he married Susan. I won't come between a man and his wife, even if I was married to him first."

Sage thought of all the nights she'd heard her mother cry herself to sleep through the thin wall dividing their bedrooms. Her mother had tried to be strong, to hide her pain, but even at six years old, Sage knew something awful had happened. And that nothing would be the same.

"Do you ever wish you'd never married him in the first place? That you could go back and avoid the heartache?"

"Never," her mother answered instantly. "Each tear I shed for your father, I would willingly shed ten times over for even one of your smiles." Her mom gently touched her cheek. "You are my greatest blessing, honeybee."

Knowing she meant every word, Sage wrapped her arms around her mother's neck, burying her face in her shoulder-length curls.

As she breathed in her homey, herbal scent, and caught CeCe's smile over her shoulder, Sage could hear Flynn's voice as he described *The Curious Quest of Quinley Culpepper* yesterday morning in *Mira*'s galley.

I realized it's about the journey of finding yourself.

He'd been so right. The story wasn't about the search for one person to fill a void. It had more to do with the search for oneself, who God made us to be—whole, complete, and unique, in Him. And about how He brings people into our lives—people like her mom and Gran and CeCe and so many others—to be our family.

Hidden behind a tale of mystery and adventure was a profound truth. A truth she hadn't fully embedded in her heart until that moment.

There had been a time she'd let Flynn become her whole world. Her only source of happiness. And when he left, she'd lost everything.

Or so she'd thought.

But her family was here all along, both her anchors and her sails, given her need.

And she never wanted to lose sight of that blessing again.

Chapter 31

FLYNN

FLYNN ROOTED around in the closet of his childhood bedroom where the belongings he'd left behind had been stashed when he'd moved out. Although all his stuff had been stacked in boxes, the decor of his bedroom had largely remained unchanged. And why wouldn't it? The large suite facing the ocean had been decked out by an interior designer from day one, with age-appropriate tweaks as he'd grown older.

For the most part, he didn't mind that his room resembled a Ralph Lauren catalog. His sailing and regatta posters blended into the nautical theme so well, his mother barely even wrinkled her nose at his unauthorized additions. Although she did occasionally complain about the marks in the wall from all the push pins.

Aha! There it is.

Flynn found the Ziploc bag buried beneath worn copies of *Dove* and *Sailing Alone around the World*.

He crawled out of the closet and sat on the floor beside Cap, who happily chewed on the old baseball from middle school Flynn kept before he'd realized he was much better at tennis. "Enjoy that primo leather, buddy. Knowing Dad, that ball cost no less than a hundred bucks."

Cap raised his bushy eyebrows, then resumed his contented gnawing, clearly unimpressed.

Flynn unzipped the plastic baggie, releasing the earthy scent of old paper and thread. He closed his eyes and breathed deeper, basking in the comforting aroma. So much better than the fake-smelling fragrance of whatever air freshener his mother had the housekeeper use to keep the empty rooms from turning musty. Why spritz imitation ocean breeze when the *actual* ocean was right outside your window?

Flynn slowly opened his eyes and forced himself to study the contents of the baggie. His heartbeat picked up speed, like a sloop's sail catching the wind.

The familiar gut-wrenching weight of guilt crashed into him.

Two items, so simple on the surface.

A benign slip of paper and a braided friendship bracelet.

Innocuous except for the harsh reality that they shouldn't be here, in this house, in his hands.

They should be in a watertight trinket box, wedged in a very specific crevice in Coyote Cave. A crevice his brother had specially selected ten years ago, when he first had the idea for the time capsule.

Flynn scrunched his eyes shut again, pained by the memories bombarding him from all sides. His throat clenched, making it difficult to breathe.

Man up. Don't wimp out now. It's time you finally faced this.

As if sensing his distress, Cap nudged his hand.

Flynn opened his eyes, and gave Cap's head a gentle pat. "Don't worry, bud. I'm fine. Or at least, I will be. This is something I've been needing to do for a long time." With a fortifying breath, he removed the slip of paper and smoothed out the haphazard folds.

His youthful handwriting filled the page.

It had been ten years since he'd penned the letter. And he couldn't remember a single word he'd written.

"Well, younger self, what gems of wisdom do you have for me?" he asked aloud, more nervous than he'd expected to finally read his decade-old words.

Dear Future Flynn,

I don't really understand why Kev insisted we do this. I guess it's something he read about in one of those self-help books for wannabe billionaires. He has about every book on business ever written. And he's read them each ten times. I don't know why he tries so hard. He was born to be a big success. I bet those twelve extra minutes of life ensured he got all the overachiever genes.

But, hey. I'm not complaining. I'll gladly stand in the shadows and cheer him on. All I want is to be with Sage and to sail. So, ten years from now, I just want to be doing what I love with the woman I love.

His heart ached at his naive optimism.

When he wrote the letter, he couldn't imagine a life

without Sage. Or his brother. Then, in the span of a single summer, he'd lost them both.

I may not know The 7 Habits of Highly Effective People *or* Who Moved My Cheese, *but I've always liked this quote by Robin Lee Graham. The guy's a legend. And considering he sailed around the world at only 16, I think he knows a thing or two.*

Robin Lee Graham said, "At sea, I learned how little a person needs, not how much."

That pretty much sums up how I feel, too. I said something similar to Mom once, and she gave me the strangest look. I swear, if Kev and I weren't identical, she'd be banging down the door of the hospital, claiming they gave her the wrong kid.

Anyway, I don't really need to write my future self a letter. And I don't really need to put my most prized possession in a time capsule to remind me what's important in ten years.

Kev may worry about losing focus as he gets older. That can happen when you're busy taking over the world and whatnot.

But not me. I don't need tricks or trends like time capsules.

I won't lose sight of who I am.

So, my best advice to my future self?

Keep doing what you're doing and enjoy the ride.

Flynn winced at his own words.

You have no idea how wrong you are.

He lifted the bracelet from the bag—the one Sage made, with a matching pair for her and Kev to symbolize their immortal friendship. His most prized possession. A reminder of the two people closest to him in the whole world.

What had Kevin chosen as his item? What had he written to his future self?

He'd considered opening the time capsule countless times over the years. Even more so as the ten-year marker approached. But he couldn't bring himself to go back there. To the place where his brother died. *Because of him.*

A cold chill swept over him, penetrating all the way to his marrow.

He couldn't let his brother's memories languish in that cave. Kev wasn't here to retrieve the time capsule, which meant Flynn would have to go instead.

But he wouldn't have to do it alone.

Flynn raked a fidgety hand through his hair. Should he really do this? Should he invite Sage into the dark places of his past?

He'd vowed never to tell her what really happened that night. He didn't want her to carry a single ounce of guilt, especially since it wasn't her fault. It was his own burden to bear.

But he saw the damage he'd caused by leaving, when, at the time, he thought he was doing the right thing. Maybe he needed to change his mind about this well-intentioned decision, too?

He slipped the bracelet over his wrist and cinched it tight, resolute in his new plan.

He'd tell Sage the truth. The whole truth. And he'd do it tonight.

But first, he needed to have a conversation with his parents.

It wouldn't be pleasant. But it was necessary.

Apprehension mingled with determination as he strode across the expansive back lawn toward the white marquee tent rustling in the wind. His parents stood underneath, speaking to one of the catering staff, the stunning panoramic view of the Pacific Ocean as a backdrop.

The two minutes it took his parents to wrap up their conversation with the caterer felt like an eternity. By the time they'd turned to face him, adrenaline had kicked his pulse into overdrive.

"Hi, sweetheart. Everything is coming together beautifully for your big night." His mother beamed proudly at all her posh party details, like the illuminated lighthouse ice sculpture and enormous floral centerpieces with—*wait*. Were those live goldfish in the glass vases?

He cleared his throat, trying to concentrate on his mission. "About that. I need to talk to you and Dad about something." He swallowed. His mouth had gone from dry as sand to suddenly producing way too much saliva.

Get it together, man. It's now or never.

He filled his lungs with crisp, salty air for courage. Expelling it slowly, he ripped off the proverbial Band-Aid. "I've decided to postpone the promotion."

"You what?" His dad's eyes narrowed, and his tone took on a stern, icy quality. The kind that would silence him instantly as a kid. "You don't want to be vice president?"

"Don't get all worked up, Randolph." His mother rested a hand on his dad's arm. "I'm sure that's not what he meant."

"Actually, Mom. It is. I want to put off the promotion. In fact—" Hesitating, he cracked his knuckles. The staccato pop filled the heavy silence while he summoned his nerve. "I want to take a sabbatical from Cahill Enterprises."

His mother inhaled a horrified gasp as if he'd just confessed to living a double life as a hardened criminal.

"Absolutely not," his dad said brusquely. "Conversation closed."

"The conversation may be closed, but I haven't changed my mind. This is happening, Dad. But I'm not quitting. I'm just taking a break to pursue something else for a while." Although, he had a feeling returning to work for his father at the end of his sabbatical would be even harder than he thought.

"This is because of *her*, isn't it?" his mother hissed with poorly suppressed outrage.

"It's my decision," Flynn said firmly, trying to keep Sage away from the firing line.

"You may think it is, but that girl has cast a spell on you. Whatever they're doing at the place with their bees and herbs, it's borderline witchcraft."

"Come on, Mom," he groaned at her obvious exaggeration. "You know it's not. And if you keep saying stuff like that about Sage and her family, I'll leave right now and we won't come to the gala tonight."

"We?" Her eyes widened.

"Yes, Mom. *We*. Sage is coming. And I'm asking you to please end your ridiculous war against her."

His mother lifted her chin ever so slightly, but didn't say another word.

Was it his imagination or were her eyes wet with tears?

"This gala is about more than your promotion," his father interjected, ever the voice of calm reason. "It's the forty-year anniversary of Cahill Enterprises. You've been a big part of the company, so I'd still like you to come on stage with me and your mother during my speech. We'll discuss your *decision* later." The way his father said the word *decision*, he might as well have used air quotes.

Flynn should've known he wouldn't be able to skate by with one conversation on the subject.

But he'd worry about that later.

Tonight, he simply wanted to enjoy the evening with the woman he loved and make up for lost time.

Chapter 32

ABBY

ABBY STOOD ON THE SHORE, her back to the world, the open water stretched out before her. She dug her toes into the silky sand, basking in the warm sun against her skin and the cool wind in her hair.

Several feet up the embankment, the inn bustled with daily life. Sadie and Lucy rested from their travels, settling in their rooms and enjoying their luxury welcome baskets. Piper helped Logan prepare dinner—which would be interesting since neither one of them could cook—and Max and Tyler played with Ron, Max's pet rabbit, in the sitting room.

Somehow, life went on, ebbing and flowing like the tide, even as she sank deeper into the abyss of heartache and confusion.

Donnie had an affair. She knew that for certain now.

No, they hadn't been married yet, but how much did that really matter? She'd committed to him, heart and soul. She's trusted in his faithfulness. And he'd betrayed her.

Please, tell her that I love her. And that I'm sorry.

Donnie's words tumbled in her mind, consuming her

every thought. They simultaneously sliced her heart and soothed it, leaving her more torn than ever.

An amber glint in the wet sand caught her eye. Rushing into the foamy surf, she plunged her hand into the icy water before the receding tide reclaimed its treasure.

As the wave retreated back to sea, Abby returned to higher ground and perched on a driftwood log to examine her prize.

A tiny pebble of orange sea glass rested in her palm, pure and stunning, like a small slice of the sun.

Although she'd seen the unusual hue in art and jewelry, she'd never glimpsed the gorgeous rarity in the wild. According to Sage, who'd made her a beautiful sea glass tree topper last Christmas, orange was the least common color, since very little orange glass was ever produced.

For a moment, Abby merely stared at the opaque stone, marveling at its rounded edges. How could something as jagged and razor-sharp as broken glass become so perfectly smooth?

She wasn't sure if it was the unexpected beauty of the sea glass that moved her or the emotions of the day over-whelming her once again, but tears sprang to her eyes. She let them gather on her lashes, magnifying the stone's ruddy hue.

"Oh, that's lovely." Verna's voice carried over her shoulder, startling Abby from her thoughts. "And orange! That's a rare find."

Verna let Bing off his leash to waddle in the surf and sat on the log beside her. The sun sank lower in the sky, staining the water lavender and pink.

"Is everything all right, dear?" Verna asked when she noticed Abby's tears.

"No," Abby sniffled. "Sadly, it's not. And I don't know if it will ever be all right again." She unburdened her sorrow, sharing everything that transpired earlier that afternoon.

Verna listened silently, except for the occasional murmurs of sympathy and surprise.

By the time Abby finally finished her sordid tale, Verna was dabbing her own tears with the edge of her purple scarf. "I'm so sorry, sweetheart. I'd prayed it wasn't true."

"Me, too." Abby lifted her gaze from the sea glass to glimpse the sunset splashed across the ocean waves. So many vibrant colors, like a painter's canvas, interspersed with streaks of liquid gold. The striking beauty contrasted so harshly against the ugliness in her heart, tears sprang anew.

"I'm so angry, Verna," she confessed in a hoarse whisper. "I'm angry at Donnie for what he did. And I'm even angrier that he's not here to take the brunt of my anger, which probably makes no sense at all." She roughly wiped her damp cheeks with her clenched fist, her fingers still wound tightly around the sea glass. "And I'm angry with myself. Because I want to forgive him so badly, but I don't know if I should. I don't want to be weak."

Verna sat beside her in silence for a long moment before saying softly, "In my experience, forgiveness isn't a weakness. It's a sign of great strength. But then, forgiveness isn't what some people think. It isn't denial. And it isn't being a door-mat. Forgiveness isn't some passive thing. It's active. And powerful. And it impacts the forgiver a lot more than the offender."

"If I forgive him, will all this pain go away?" *Please, please tell me it will go away.*

"Probably not. Not at first. The wound will feel raw for a

while, sharp and ragged around the edges. Much like that piece of glass once did." She nodded toward Abby's tightly coiled fist.

Abby slowly unfurled her fingers, bathing the frosted glass in soft, ethereal light.

"It takes years for the sea and sand to work its magic, polishing and refining to produce such a stunning transformation."

"Years?" Abby whimpered. She wanted relief right this second, not years from now.

"No one can say exactly how long heartache or hardship will last. But you know what sea glass always reminds me of?" Verna didn't wait for a response before answering her own question. "Isaiah 43:2, when the Lord says to His people, 'When you pass through the waters, I will be with you.' That's a promise. To me and to you."

Abby watched the waves slip back to sea, and thanks to Verna's reassuring words, some of her grief and anger vanished with it. She leaned her head against the older woman's shoulder, savoring the way her softly scented perfume mingled with the salty ocean air. Somewhere along the way, this woman had become as much a mother to her as her own. "Thank you, Verna."

"My pleasure, dear one." Verna patted her hand that held the sea glass. "Now, don't you lose that. It's very special."

"I won't." Abby slipped it into her pocket.

The sea glass would serve as a sign. A sign to forgive. And a sign for the future.

Thanks to Verna, she knew exactly what she needed to do next.

She needed to call Victor.

SAGE

Sage took in her elegant surroundings with an air of disbelief. The Cahill gardens resembled a magical fairyland, with lush, fragrant flowers and twinkling lights everywhere.

She'd expected her presence to provoke some snide comments or passive-aggressive remarks from Cordelia or, at the very least, some withering glances. But Flynn's mother had been perfectly civil, bordering on pleasant.

In fact, the entire evening had passed like a dream. Dancing, incredible food, and stunning views of the sunset from the clifftop estate.

Flynn hadn't left her side all evening, except to fetch them a fresh glass of champagne.

She smiled, her heart soaring with unbridled bliss, as he wove through the gathering of impeccably dressed guests, wielding two crystal flutes.

He passed her a glass, and up close, she noticed the worry lines creasing his brow.

"What's wrong?" Had his mother's good mood finally worn off?

"Nothing. It's just—there's something I need to tell you." His frown lines deepened, and her pulse sputtered.

"What is it?" She managed to keep her voice steady while her heartbeat thrummed wildly.

"It's something important. But we can't talk here. It needs to be somewhere private." He glanced toward the house. The regal mansion with its myriad windows and multiple balconies gleamed in the darkness. "Can we go inside for a minute?"

She swallowed the bitter taste of panic. What did he want to talk about? It sounded serious. Had he changed his mind about the sailing charter? About *them*?

Relax. Breathe. You're jumping to the worst-case scenario. Flynn wouldn't do that to you. Not again.

"Sure." She tried to keep her voice from shaking as she set her unsipped champagne on the tray of a passing server.

But before they could move toward the house, Randolph Cahill's commanding voice reverberated across the garden.

"Thank you all for coming tonight." Tall and imposing in a slick black suit, Randolph stood on a raised podium, Cordelia preening by his side. He caught Flynn's eye, and an unspoken directive passed between father and son.

"Will you excuse me for one second? I'll be right back." He handed her his glass of champagne and kissed her cheek before heading toward the podium.

She watched him walk away, a sinking feeling in the pit of her stomach.

You're being ridiculous. Everything is fine.

She took a sip of Flynn's champagne.

"Today marks the fortieth anniversary of our little family

company, and we couldn't be prouder of how far we've come."

Sage tried not to roll her eyes at his self-deprecating tone. The *little family company* had hundreds of employees.

As Randolph launched into a well-rehearsed speech about how he'd founded the business from nothing, *yada, yada, yada,* Sage glanced around at the mingling guests, wondering how many times they'd heard the same story. And how much of it had been exaggerated over the years.

"Of course, I couldn't have done any of it without my wife and partner, Cordelia." At this part of the speech, Cordelia offered the crowd a self-effacing smile, as if she had no idea she'd be recognized by her husband.

Sage took another sip of champagne.

"I'd also like to thank my son."

The champagne fizz burned the back of her throat, and she pressed a fist to her chest, both to clear the tingling bubbles and calm her racing heart.

"Thanks to Flynn's tireless dedication over the last decade, we surpassed our company goals year after year." Randolph placed a proud hand on Flynn's shoulder.

Sage stretched onto her tiptoes, straining for a better look at Flynn's face, desperate to read his indiscernible expression. Was he nervous? Uncomfortable? Anxious for the ordeal to be over?

"Which is why," Cordelia interjected, taking the microphone from her husband's hands, "we're thrilled to announce Flynn's new role as vice president of Cahill Enterprises, effective immediately."

As Cordelia beamed like a beacon from the podium, the crowd erupted in applause.

Sage staggered backward, sloshing champagne onto her shoes.

No. This couldn't be happening. Flynn had given her his word.

The world seemed to spin and spiral out of control, and everything turned upside down.

Suddenly, she was eighteen again, waiting on a dock for someone who'd never arrive. Abandoned. Discarded. Like she'd never mattered at all.

The heat of humiliation singed her skin.

This is what he wanted to talk about, what he'd wanted to tell her.

All night long, he'd known this would happen.

They'd laughed together, held hands, and stolen secret kisses.

She'd never felt more foolish or so agonizingly disoriented.

Desperate to escape, she set the champagne flute on the ledge of a stone planter and scrambled up the back steps into the house. She bumped into a server with a fresh tray of hors d'oeuvres exiting through the French doors. Mumbling an apology, she kept her head down, embarrassed by the mounting tears poised to tumble down her cheeks any moment.

She made it out the front door, down the marble steps, and onto the gravel drive before she heard Flynn's voice.

"Sage, wait!" he called after her, urgent and breathless.

"I did wait for you," she shouted back without looking over her shoulder or slowing her pace. "For five excruciating hours, I waited on that dock for you." Bleary-eyed, she followed the faint glow of pathway lights lining the sloping drive.

"Please, Sage. You don't understand." His voice drew closer, and she kicked off her heels, leaving them behind as she quickened her pace, ignoring the prick of pebbles beneath her bare feet.

"You're the one who doesn't understand." Hurt and frustration rose in her chest, crowding out her lungs, suffocating all rational thought, leaving only her raw emotions. Whirling around, she asked, "Do you have any idea what those five hours were like for me? I thought something horrible had happened to you. I thought I'd lost you, too." Her voice broke as the memory of that day barged into her thoughts. She'd never been more terrified, convinced nothing but an awful act of fate could keep him from meeting her that day.

A sob welled in her throat, and she bit the inside of her cheek to keep it at bay, determined not to break down in front of him.

"I'm so sorry." He stood beside her now, his tone an avalanche of remorse.

She couldn't bring herself to look at his face, to see the emotion in his eyes. Pain and confusion mixed with the past and present, leaving her a muddled mess. She suddenly needed him to know exactly what she went through that day. "I went to your house after you didn't show up, to see if you were okay. Your mom told me you'd left. She said you finally came to your senses and didn't want anything to do with me anymore."

"I'm sorry she said that to you." Flynn sounded genuinely pained by his mother's words, but Sage couldn't see past her own blinding hurt. "You know it wasn't true, right?"

"And how would I know that?" Pain clawed at her chest, desperate to escape in a weep or a whimper, anything to release the pressure crushing her heart. "You didn't call. You didn't write. You simply left. You let your dad use his money and connections to get you into Wharton in Kevin's place, and then you just disappeared from my life without a word."

She glanced up at the stars, blinking rapidly to delay the burgeoning tears.

Whatever you do, do not cry in front of him.

"I'm so s—"

"Don't!" She held up a trembling hand. "Don't say you're sorry. I'm tired of your *I'm sorrys* when nothing ever changes. The last time you left, I fell apart. But not this time. This time will be different." Her voice shook, and she gathered a steadying breath. "This time, I'm the one leaving. And I don't want you to follow me." The words left her mouth like sharp, unflinching stabs, meant to leave a mark.

She quickly spun around and resumed her trek down the hill before he could spot the tears falling freely now.

Music and laughter from the party trailed after her, blending with the crunch of gravel beneath her throbbing feet and the gentle hum of the distant sea.

But there was one sound she didn't hear.

The sound of Flynn coming after her.

Despite her attempt at self-preservation, to fend off more pain, the deafening silence hurt as much in that moment as it had ten years ago when she stood alone on that dock.

Chapter 34

FLYNN

FLYNN STOOD FROZEN in agonizing indecision.

Should I go after her?

Every fiber in his being ached to rush after Sage, to explain the misunderstanding. His mother had acted on her own, trying to pressure him into taking the promotion. But it wouldn't work. He hadn't changed his mind.

But what if Sage wasn't ready to talk? What if she needed more time?

He wavered, afraid to push her too hard too soon and ruin his chances at mending the rift.

But the thought of Sage walking down the hill alone, climbing into her car and heading home, thinking he'd betrayed her was too much for him to bear.

He started down the hill after her.

"You're making a mistake," his mother called after him. "You should let her go."

Indignation fired in his chest, and he swung around. "How could you do that to me? You had no right. I told you I wasn't accepting the promotion."

"I'm your mother. I don't want to see you throw your life away for some girl."

"Sage isn't *some girl*. And it's not my life, is it? It's Kevin's." His fingers tensed, and he curled them into fists by his sides to steady his rising emotion. "That's what this is really about, isn't it? I'm a carbon copy of your favorite son, and you can't bear the thought I might become *me* again. The family embarrassment. The son who will never amount to anything."

She flinched as if he'd struck her. "Sweetheart, no. Is that what you think?" The shock and dismay in her voice surprised him.

"I heard you, Mom. The day of Kevin's funeral. 'Please, God. Anyone but our Kevin.' Be honest. You would rather Kev was the one standing here, not me."

The words burned the back of his throat, but he felt a strange bittersweet relief finally forcing the truth out in the open.

"Oh, honey." In the dim light of the circular drive, her glassy eyes glistened like dark pools of water. "I'm so sorry. I was grieving. I didn't mean—" Her voice fell away, strangled by a raspy sob.

Flynn stared at her in stunned silence, shaken by the intensity of her reaction. She'd wept for Kevin, but he never imagined he could evoke the same level of feeling.

"I never wanted you to be your brother." Tears slid down her cheeks like ice melting in the moonlight. "Maybe, sometimes, I wished you were a bit more like Kevin. But only because he was easier for me to understand. You and I, we've always been so different."

Flynn couldn't argue. He'd felt the disconnect even as a

217

child. His mother could be controlling and exacting. There was one correct way to do something, and he rarely got it right. He'd even go as far to describe her as cold, although, as an adult, he'd learned to admire her strength and tenacity. In *some* situations, at least.

But tonight, in her severe black dress, her hair combed into a tight updo, she looked thinner than usual. Pale and fragile, as if her essence had fled through her fingertips, leaving only a shell.

There was only one other time he'd witnessed her impervious exterior crack.

When Kevin died.

"I've always been afraid to lose you," she admitted softly. "To either the sea and your dream of sailing around the world, or to Sage, who understood you so much better than I ever did. Then, when we lost your brother, that fear consumed me. I would do anything in my power to keep from losing you, too." She slumped forward, drained and defeated, as if she finally realized she'd been fighting a hopeless battle.

"Is that why you've always treated Sage so poorly?"

"Yes." The syllable escaped in a strained whisper. She rubbed her eyes, smearing her mascara, although she didn't appear to notice or care. "I'm sorry, sweetheart. Despite how it may seem sometimes, I'm not proud of what I've done."

As her words sank in, he struggled to accept them. He wanted to offer his mother compassion, but he couldn't help a lingering resentment for all the times she'd lashed out at Sage. Sage, who'd never been anything but polite and respectful in return. "The person who deserves the apology is Sage."

"I know." She sniffled, wiping her nose with the back of her hand—the most unladylike gesture he'd ever seen her do. "I'll apologize for every unkind word I've ever said."

"And for the bookstore." Another spark of indignation flashed inside him. He still couldn't believe she'd stooped so low. "Why'd you do it, Mom? We weren't even dating anymore."

She hesitated. Uncertainty swam in her tearful gaze as she chewed her bottom lip, ruining her expertly applied lipstick. After a tormenting pause, she released a resigned, remorseful breath, as if she knew her confession might push him even further away. "Because I knew how badly she wanted to open her own bookstore, and I thought if she couldn't do it here, in Blessings Bay, because of the bylaw, then she might move and start a new life somewhere else. And I could finally let go of the fear that one day she'd take you away from me."

Flynn winced. Because of him, his mother had destroyed Sage's dream. And tonight, he may have ruined any hope she had of making a second attempt.

"I'm so sorry." Tears tumbled down his mother's face, leaving inky-black streaks of mascara in their wake. "What I did was awful. Unforgivable. I wish I could go back and change it. All of it. You and Kevin—you boys are everything to me. My heart and soul. And the day your brother—" Her voice caught, and his perpetually put together mother unraveled right before his eyes.

His heart wrenched.

Hunched over in the dim shadows, her faultless facade fell away, revealing a small, broken woman.

He moved to her side and wrapped his arm around her trembling shoulders.

She released a quivering breath and leaned against him.

Years of reprehensible behavior couldn't be erased in a single night, but an ounce of understanding went a long way toward repairing the wound on his heart.

For the first time, he could see a clear path forward.

A path to mend his broken family.

And a path to start a new family with Sage.

If he could earn her forgiveness first.

Chapter 35

SAGE

SAGE SAT BACK on her heels while Gran removed the small trap on the side of the brood box where the bees deposited their pollen. Early afternoon sunlight bathed the garden in a warm, burnished glow, as if offering her hopeful assurance that the new day would ease the pain of last night.

As if that were even possible.

In less than twenty-four hours, she'd lost Flynn. Their partnership. The boat. Her best chance to finally open her bookstore.

And the worst part? She knew she should accept what happened and move on. She needed to be like her mom and Gran, and every woman who came to the Honeybee Retreat. She needed to put the broken pieces of her life back together and build a better future for herself. Without Flynn.

And yet, despite the knowledge that life would go on without him—that she'd be okay—she missed him so much her whole body ached. And she couldn't help wondering if walking away had been a horrible mistake.

Her phone hummed in the side pocket of her long

cotton skirt, but she ignored the vibration for the hundredth time that day.

Flynn hadn't stopped calling since last night. And texting. And leaving countless voicemails.

But she couldn't bring herself to look at her phone, too afraid her resolve would slip.

She wanted to forgive him, to grasp at any excuse to give him another chance. But what would that say about her? That she was weak? That she'd given a man too much power over her heart again?

An image of her father crouched on the worn carpet in their old house, his bags stacked by the front door, crept into her thoughts. He'd tugged on one of her pigtails and teased, *Why the sad face, kiddo? We'll still see each other all the time.*

She'd clung to that promise for far too long, desperate to believe him. The first Christmas after he left, she wouldn't let her mom put the star on the tree, convinced he'd show up to carry on the tradition. The top of the tree remained bare that year.

On her seventh birthday, she'd made her mother wait to cut the cake. It sat in the fridge for ten days until speckles of mold mingled with the rainbow sprinkles.

Countless times, she'd given her father the benefit of the doubt. Until one day, her well of faith ran dry. She only wished it hadn't taken so long.

Her phone buzzed again, harmonizing with the hum of the honeybees.

"Maybe you should get that before it vibrates a hole right through your pocket," Gran teased, scooping the pollen pellets into a glass jar.

"It's probably Flynn again." She let it go to voicemail.

"Why don't you want to answer it? Did something happen last night?" Gran slid the thin drawer back into the brood box.

Sage winced. She still hadn't told her mom and Gran what happened. Saying the words aloud would lend a note of finality she wasn't ready to face.

"I just think it might be time for me to move on and focus on my future. I don't need Flynn, or any man, to live a fulfilling life."

She vocalized her thoughts for her own benefit as much as Gran's, but even though she believed the statement, her chest constricted.

You have your friends and family. And that will always be enough.

Gran knelt on her padded gardening mat in thoughtful silence as honeybees danced around her.

"That's true," Gran said slowly. The bees darted to and fro, dispersing in different directions as she nodded her head. "Being single is a blessing. For many reasons. But so is finding your person and going through life together as a team." A honeybee perched on her shoulder, a willing audience to her wisdom. "A man shouldn't be your whole world. But he can be an important part of it. As long as you choose wisely."

"And how do you know you've chosen wisely?" The expression *blinded by love* had become a cliché for a reason. And both her mother and Gran had married men they'd loved only to be betrayed and abandoned.

"'Look not at a ship's prow, with its intricate carvings and figureheads, or its lustrous sails. Instead, look to the wake it leaves behind.'"

Sage blinked, startled by the quote from her favorite

book. Had everyone read *The Curious Quest of Quinley Culpepper*?

Gran's eyes twinkled.

Although she'd quoted the passage out of context, Sage guessed what her grandmother meant. What did Flynn's life say about his character?

She thought of his love and loyalty toward his brother and the way he cared for Cap. And even though his parents could be exasperating, Flynn treated them with respect. And what about the way he'd treated her? Giving her the bed without a second thought. Taking care of her after her fall. Reading her favorite book simply to be close to her.

Her fingertips tingled at the memory of his touch, the night they'd fallen asleep holding hands—the night he'd apologized for the past.

Had he meant the words he'd whispered in the darkness?

Was it possible last night had been a misunderstanding after all?

Her phone buzzed again.

She jumped, startled from her reverie.

Should she answer it? If she let Flynn back into her life, she'd be chancing another broken heart.

Was a future with Flynn worth the risk?

Her heart fluttering with apprehension, she reached into her pocket for her phone.

"Ouch!" A sharp prick pierced her finger. As she withdrew her hand, a twitching honeybee tumbled to the ground.

"Oh, no! The poor dear." Dismayed, Gran scooped the crumpled little body into her palm.

"I'm sorry, Gran. I didn't realize she had crawled into my pocket." Wincing, Sage plucked the stinger from her flesh.

Growing up at the Honeybee Retreat, she'd been stung before. And she'd been taught to treat the helpful pollinators with care and understanding, not fear. A bee only stung when threatened. And it cost the creature its life, versus the few seconds of pain she endured.

"It's not your fault. These things happen. It's just such a shame. I wish we could communicate better, to let them know we're not a threat. To think, a simple misunderstanding—a rash reaction out of fear—cost this little bee everything."

Gran sniffled, cradling the lifeless bundle of black and yellow with the utmost care and sympathy.

Sage watched as honeybees converged around them, responding to the pheromones released with the stinger.

In the bee's death, she'd sent her hive a warning of a potential threat.

And, in a way, she'd sent Sage a warning, too.

Sometimes, a miscommunication could cost you more than you realized.

Chapter 36

ABBY

"ABBY, these waffles are incredible. Thick and fluffy with just the right amount of sweetness." Lucy Gardener shoveled an enormous forkful into her mouth, closed her eyes, and groaned with delight as if she hadn't eaten in weeks.

"Thank you. I'm so happy you're enjoying them." Abby refilled Lucy's coffee cup, trying not to gawk as the statuesque woman scarfed down a slice of bacon in two bites. She struggled to reconcile the stunning blonde's slender, angelic figure with her hearty appetite. But then, as a petite woman who loved food, she should know better than to make assumptions.

Sadie must have noticed her staring because she smiled and said, "Don't mind her. She's been on a restrictive diet for over a year trying to find the cause of her migraines."

"Turns out I'm allergic to a rare chemical used in a certain type of polyester," Lucy added between bites. "My wardrobe will take a small hit, but I can finally enjoy food again." With a thoughtful pause, she tapped the fork tines to her lips. "Which, now that I think about it, may not be great for fitting into my wedding dress." She shrugged and gave a pleasant, lighthearted laugh before digging into her waffles again.

Abby smiled. Upon their arrival yesterday, she immediately liked her new guests. Sadie seemed like a down-to-earth realist compared to Lucy's chipper optimism, but both women were sweet and warmhearted. The kind of women Abby would happily befriend. The one downside? Thanks to the constant chatter about their upcoming double wedding, Abby's thoughts frequently wandered to Logan's almost-proposal. That is, *if* he'd been about to propose. She still wasn't sure if she'd misread the situation.

Either way, the possibility of an impending engagement made her realize how badly she wanted to marry Logan. Yes, the thought had crossed her mind many times before, but she'd always brushed it off, convinced it was far too soon to even consider. She'd dated Donnie for three years before he proposed. She and Logan had been together less than six months.

They should wait... shouldn't they?

"How long were you each with your fiancés before you got engaged?" she asked impulsively, topping off Sadie's strawberry-hibiscus tea.

The two best friends exchanged glances then grinned.

"Less than a year," Sadie told her. "Lucy started dating Vick in the fall and then Landon and I got together that winter. Then we both got engaged the following spring."

"Feels like only yesterday *and* a lifetime ago," Lucy added with a dreamy glow about her. "What about you, Abby? How long have you been married?"

"Oh. I'm not—I mean, we're not— We're just dating,"

Abby stammered, her cheeks flushed. Why did that question always catch her off guard? Possibly because she wanted it to be true.

"Sorry." Lucy flashed a sheepish grimace. "I should have looked for a ring. You two just seem so in sync, I assumed you've been happily married for years."

"It does feel that way sometimes," Abby admitted. Whether they'd been together six months or six years, she couldn't imagine life without Logan. Her heart had made its choice ages ago. Logan was her person. And she'd choose him a million times over. Her intuition told her that Logan felt the same way. Was he worried all the drama with Piper would mar their special moment?

As if on cue, a throat cleared. Piper lingered in the doorway of the dining room. "Sorry to interrupt. I'm heading to Verna's to pick up Tyler, and then we're taking off."

Abby's heartbeat stuttered. *It's time.* "Would you ladies excuse me for a second?"

"Of course," Sadie said while Lucy nodded, her mouth full again. "It was nice to meet you, Piper. Thank you for the delicious snickerdoodles. Lucy and I have enjoyed several already."

Lucy swallowed, then exchanged her own goodbye with Piper before Abby stepped into the hall.

"Before you go, I have something for you." Her pulse whirring, Abby led Piper to the sitting room. As she reached into the top drawer of the vintage campaign desk, she caught a glimpse of Logan, Max, and Tyler playing in Verna's front yard across the street.

The boys looked so happy, so carefree. Logan was a

wonderful father. A wonderful man. And they'd built a beautiful life together.

A wave of gratitude crashed into her, and she swallowed against the sudden tightness in her throat. Turning toward Piper, she handed her an envelope.

"Oh. Thank you, but Logan already paid me." Piper tried to pass it back.

"It's not the money you earned."

"What is it?" Piper slid out a stack of papers, frowning at all the legal jargon.

"It's a trust for Tyler. There's money to go toward everyday expenses and more that he'll receive when he's eighteen, either for college or whatever path he chooses."

"I—I don't understand." Piper scanned the document, looking dazed. When she finally met her gaze, tears shimmered in her eyes. "Why are you doing this?"

Abby drew in a slow, deliberate breath. She'd asked herself that question several times, and always came up with the same answer. "It's what Donnie would have wanted."

A tear tumbled down Piper's cheek, but she didn't wipe it away.

"Donnie wasn't perfect," Abby told her, fighting her own welling emotions. "And I might wrestle with what he did for a long time to come. But I believe that he loved me. And I believe he would've loved his son more than anything." Her heart squeezed. For what she lost. For what Tyler lost. But she also felt a strange release in finally putting Donnie's money to use, as if this was its intended purpose all along.

To her surprise, Piper threw her arms around her, knocking the air from her lungs. "Thank you, thank you, thank you," she murmured, her tears dampening Abby's hair.

As Piper wept on her shoulder, Abby exhaled, letting her bitterness seep to the floor.

Forgiveness isn't a weakness. It's a sign of great strength. And it impacts the forgiver a lot more than the offender.

Verna's words rang in her ear, clear and sweet and true.

Sniffling, Piper pulled back and wiped her eyes to study the papers again. "I—I still can't believe it. What can I do to repay your kindness?"

"You don't need to do anything. The money is yours, no strings attached. But—" Abby hesitated. Was she about to ask for too much? Was it a terrible idea?

"What is it?" Piper prompted.

Abby tucked a strand of hair behind her ear, wavering. *Just say it.* Taking another deep breath, she asked, "Would it be okay if we stayed in touch? I know Max would really like to be in Tyler's life. And... so would I."

Piper blinked, as if Abby's question was the last one she'd anticipated. "I—Yes. I—I would like that, too."

They stood in awkward silence for a moment, gazing at each other as if neither knew what to say.

Abby felt an odd urge to hug her again, but she had something else to say—something that would most likely kill the convivial mood. "There's one more thing." She bit her bottom lip, bracing for the bad news. "I spoke to a friend at the sheriff's office and explained your situation with your landlord."

Piper opened her mouth to protest, so Abby quickly added, "I didn't give your name or any personal details. But I wanted to see what kind of charges you'd be facing if you turned yourself in."

"And?" Piper asked warily.

"It looks like you'd get off with a warning. Especially if you agree to testify against your landlord."

Piper didn't respond but appeared to be mulling over her words.

For good measure, Abby added, "It's your decision. But I think it would be the right thing to do."

"Maybe. I'll think about it," Piper relented, then sighed. "Sounds like I have a lot of tough decisions to make. Like where to go next. And what to do with my life now that Tyler and I can afford a fresh start."

"What about starting over at the beginning?"

"What do you mean?"

What *did* she mean? The words had escaped before she'd had a chance to think twice. But now that she had, maybe it wasn't the worst idea. "What if you moved back to Blessings Bay?"

"Are you serious?"

"Surprisingly, yes." Abby grinned, realizing how ridiculous her suggestion sounded. "Tyler loves it here. And I hear there are part-time jobs opening at the Sawmill and CeCe's café. They're entry-level positions, but they pay well and would be stepping stones."

"I would love that. But are you sure you'd be comfortable with me living in town?"

A valid question. On some level, it would definitely be weird. But Blessings Bay had saved her life when she'd been drowning in grief. The loving, kindhearted townspeople had given her the connection and close-knit community she'd so desperately needed. They'd become her family. Something Piper and Tyler clearly lacked. "I'm sure," she said and actually meant it.

Although, Logan might take some convincing. She smiled at the thought of her sweet, slightly overprotective boyfriend. Maybe soon-to-be something more?

Piper enveloped her in another hug. "I can't thank you enough, Abby. Tyler is going to be thrilled!" She beamed, and the genuine, unguarded smile transformed her entire appearance, creating a stark contrast from the first moment they'd met.

Piper's dull, tired eyes with dark circles draped underneath now looked vibrant and sparkling. Her aura of sadness and desperation gave way to unbridled joy and hope for the future. She practically skipped toward the door, then paused.

As she turned to face her, Piper's countenance softened, becoming almost somber. "The morning Donnie left, he mumbled something under his breath. It sounded like some sort of self-chastisement. He said, 'You don't throw dirt on a diamond.'"

Abby frowned. What did that mean?

"I didn't understand what he meant until I met you," Piper admitted. "*You're* the diamond, Abby. Bright, beautiful, and unbelievably strong. And your strength stems from your kindness." Piper flashed a I-can't-believe-I'm-saying-this smile as she confessed, "I admire you, Abby Preston. More than I've ever admired anyone before. And I hope, one day, I can be more like you."

With those words, Piper slipped out the front door, leaving Abby in stunned silence.

She'd just been given the most profound compliment by the last person she'd ever expected.

And at that moment, she felt her heart take another step toward healing.

Another step toward her own new beginning.

Chapter 37

SAGE

SAGE LEFT Gran to carry out an impromptu honeybee memorial service and strode back toward the house to make her phone call to Flynn in private.

What would she say? She had no idea. Except, she finally wanted to hear his explanation surrounding what happened last night. Had he really changed his mind and accepted the promotion? Was he leaving her again?

At the possibility, her heart ached so acutely she stopped in her tracks, waiting for the pain to pass. That's when she noticed the tall, lithe man walking up the dirt driveway. He wore a vintage golf ensemble from the 1920s, complete with long argyle socks and jaunty cap. Which was odd, considering Blessings Bay didn't have a single golf course.

"Mr. Mackensie?" she greeted him in surprise. Although she'd only ever seen the man from a distance, his unusual wardrobe choices made him easy to recognize.

"Sage, hello!" He waved, smiling brightly. Up close, he looked younger than she'd expected. Early- to midseventies, maybe. Deep grooves and leathery skin from plenty of time in the sun etched his well-defined features, but even so, she would almost describe him as handsome.

His presence evoked a wave of sadness and regret, filling her thoughts with *Mira* and all her missed opportunities. What was he doing here? Was it rude to ask?

Her mother must've heard his car come up the drive because she emerged through the front door with her most welcoming smile. "Edwin, hi. What a nice surprise."

Edwin? Had they met before?

Her mother smoothed the bodice of her flowy peasant dress, looking a little flushed as she asked, "What brings you by?"

"While it's always lovely to see you, Dawn, today, I'm here to speak with your daughter."

Dawn? Always lovely to see you? Sage couldn't wrap her head around their unexpected familiarity. "You two know each other?"

"We met at an art show last month," her mother explained, smiling at Edwin.

"Your mother tossed her empty hors d'oeuvre plate in a sculpture I'd just purchased for three thousand dollars." Edwin's soft-gray eyes flickered with amusement.

Her mother's blush deepened. "I thought it was a trash can." She covered her mouth and giggled—actually *giggled*! What was going on?

"I see," Sage said slowly, although she didn't see. Not at all. Did her mother have a thing for the affluent oddball? Was the feeling mutual?

Her mom and Edwin continued to grin at each other as if sharing a private joke. Sage cleared her throat. "What did you want to speak to me about?"

"It's about *Mira*. The boat, not my late wife," he clarified, glancing at Dawn.

She smiled. "I'll go whip up some tea. Please, join me when you're done." She gestured between them, and asked, "Hot or iced?" looking only at Edwin.

"Hot, please." He watched her disappear through the front door before turning his attention to Sage. "I've come to give you this." He handed her a manila envelope.

"What is it?"

"The title to your new sailboat, of course."

"My sailboat?" Her pulse stuttered, coming to a full stop. "But it should be Flynn's boat. Technically, he found the diary."

Edwin shrugged and bent to sniff a tall stalk of lavender bordering the driveway, as if that concluded the matter.

Sage held out the envelope without opening it. "I can't accept this. It wouldn't be fair." Her arm shook as if the slip of paper inside weighed fifty pounds. What if she didn't correct Edwin's mistake? What if she accepted ownership of *Mira*? She could finally open her bookstore.

Her conscience yanked her thoughts to Kevin's bucket list.

Flynn had dedicated a decade of his life to completing the tasks. In light of the promotion, owning *Mira* was the last item to check off. Could she really take that away from him when the boat rightfully belonged to him?

Edwin straightened and studied her for a moment, his head tilted to one side. After what felt like forever, he flashed a strange, self-satisfied smile. "Well, I think my work here is done. I wonder if your mother could use some help with that tea." He moved toward the front porch.

Exasperated, Sage cried, "Wait! Did you hear what I said? The boat belongs to Flynn, not me."

One foot on the bottom step, he said, "That's funny. He said it belongs to you."

"But—but he's the one who found the diary." Why did she have to keep repeating herself? Wasn't Edwin listening? Giving up ownership of *Mira* was hard enough without having to beg the man to take the title back.

"Maybe you should open the envelope." Edwin took the rest of the steps two at a time, almost as if to prove to himself he could still do it.

Sage stared after him, completely off-kilter by the entire exchange. "Wait," she shouted again, not willing to let him walk away that easily. "Why did you do it?"

"Do what, my dear?"

"The competition. The champagne and caviar. All of it." She may have lost her dream, but that didn't mean she wasn't owed a few answers.

"Oh, that's quite simple to explain."

I doubt it, Sage thought. She doubted anything the man did was simple.

"My Mira was a bit of a matchmaker, you see. Lost love.... That plight was her favorite." His rugged features softened at the mention of his late wife. "She loved a challenge, too. You and Flynn, you two were next on her list."

"Her list?" Sage blanched. Surely there wasn't an *actual* list.

"She always said you two were the sweetest couple. Plus, Flynn shared her love of sailing, which made her even more invested in your love story. When I saw you both wanted her sailboat, it felt like a sign. I knew Mira would've wanted me to get you two back together."

Upon finally hearing the truth behind the unorthodox endeavor, Sage wasn't sure how to feel. Annoyed? Flattered? Manipulated? Grateful? There was something sweet about Edwin's tribute to his late wife. He obviously loved her dearly. But just because he had the means and opportunity didn't make it right to play with other people's lives. At least he meant well, no matter how misguided his attempt.

Although, in this case, his scheme wasn't even successful.

"I'm sorry it didn't work out the way you'd hoped," she offered, deciding to put the whole ordeal behind her.

His eyes dancing, he wrapped one hand around the door-knob. "And who says it didn't?" Without another word, he slipped inside.

Sage stood at the edge of the garden, utterly baffled. *What a bewildering man.*

When she finally gathered her wits, she opened the manila envelope. A handwritten letter rested on top of the title.

The instant she saw the familiar penmanship, her pulse fluttered in her throat like a thousand tiny wings, making it difficult to concentrate.

Sage,

I'm so sorry about last night. I don't blame you for ignoring my calls and texts, but I need you to know the truth.

My mom acted alone, against my knowledge. I

turned down the promotion. I'm not going anywhere.

I want to stay in Blessings Bay—with you.

If you'll have me.

But even if I ruined any hope of being together, there's something I need to make right.

Mira is yours. The town needs your bookstore. It needs you and your passionate belief in the power of stories.

I'd like to show you something.

If you're willing, meet me at the marina—on our dock—at noon.

I'll be waiting.

Love,

Flynn

By the time she'd read the last word, tears had muddled her vision.

He wanted her to meet him in the very spot where he'd broken her heart.

An hour ago, she wouldn't have even considered going back there.

But now? Nothing could keep her away.

Chapter 38

SAGE

Unease tapped against Sage's rib cage like the pitter-patter of raindrops on the water, rippling through her body. Her fingers and toes tingled. Her breath wobbled.

What if Flynn wasn't there?

Tentatively, she stepped onto the dock. The weathered planks creaked beneath her feet, and waves gurgled and swished below. Boats of various sizes and shapes—from cabin cruisers to fishing trawlers—filled the slips on both sides, obstructing what lay ahead.

Forcing one foot in front of the other, she made her way toward the last slip. Her legs felt heavy, as if weighed down by driftwood. When she passed a hulking catamaran previously blocking her view, her heartbeat faltered.

Flynn and Cap stood at the end of the dock, framed by *Mira* and the sparkling sea beyond.

At the soul-quenching sight—Flynn smiling and Cap wagging his tail—tears welled in her eyes and the heavy weight lifted, vanishing into the crisp, briny air above her.

Her pace quickened, her feet slapping against the

wooden slats as she broke into a run. Wind rushed past her, soft and cool against her face, ruffling her hair. Tears—first one, then two—escaped the corners of her eyes, sliding past her temples, warm against her skin.

Happy tears. Cleansing tears. Freeing, in a way she'd never felt before.

He'd waited for her, exactly as he'd promised.

Overcome with joy, all-consuming and intense, she launched herself into Flynn's arms, laughing as she cried, "You came!" She kissed him before he had a chance to respond.

He answered by pulling her close, lingering in the feel of her lips against his, familiar and sweet. He tasted like forever, like a future filled with hope.

When they finally broke apart, she couldn't stop smiling, as if her heart commanded total control of her countenance. "You're here. You actually showed up this time."

"I plan to do a whole lot more of that. Showing up for you, that is." He held her gaze, his eyes peering so deeply into hers, she momentarily lost herself in the depths of amber gold. She believed every word he said.

Cap barked, as if he didn't want to be left out.

Laughing, Sage bent to scratch behind his ears. That's when she noticed the sandwich board decorated with blue and silver balloons.

Written in white chalk were the words, *Welcome to The Unbound Bookshop: Where Stories Set Sail.*

She glanced at Flynn, barely able to believe her eyes.

"You can change the name if you don't like it." He ran his fingers through his hair in a nervous, endearing gesture. "And I have other ideas for the tagline, too. Like, *Where stories meet the open seas*. Or *Where ocean waves meet the page*. Or *Let your imagination set sail*. You get the idea."

Moved beyond words, she still couldn't speak. Her book-shop had a name. A wonderful, creative, perfect name. Suddenly, for the first time, her childhood dream felt real and tangible. It actually came true.

"You hate it? I went too far, didn't I?" Flynn asked, misreading her silence.

With fresh tears filling her eyes, she found her voice. "I love it. It's absolutely perfect. Thank you, thank you." She kissed him again, taking her time, savoring his scent, the feel of his skin beneath her fingertips.

Her bookshop wasn't the only dream coming true.

When their lips parted for the second time, he didn't let go. Holding her in his arms as if she were the most precious treasure on the planet, he tucked a wayward, windswept curl behind her ear. His gentle touch against the tender spot behind her earlobe made her shiver.

"I never stopped loving you, Sage Harper." His confession caressed the top of her head in a tone as thick and syrupy as raw honey. "Only now, my love has grown. It's rooted in the knowledge that whatever wave or storm or gale comes our way, we're stronger together." He cracked a playful smile. "I was going to use a metaphor like two sails are better than one, but then I realized that would lead to muddy waters, because, sometimes, three or more sails are even better, and accidentally extolling polygamy isn't the vibe I'm going for."

At his unexpected comment, laughter spilled to the surface, light, airy, and wonderful. She'd missed his goofy sense of humor, the way he made her feel special and cherished, as if he lived to make her smile. "I love you, too. Even when your comedic timing is terrible," she teased, so happy she might burst.

"I'll work on it." He coiled one of her curls around his finger, his knuckles gently grazing her cheek. Her heartbeat stilled at the intimacy of the gesture.

Tucked in the shade of *Mira*'s mast, surrounded by the sea and sky, she longed to stay in that moment forever. The five hours she'd stood there alone suddenly seemed so brief in light of the bigger picture, the grander story. *Their* story. And it wasn't over yet. Not even close.

A flash of blue and white around his wrist caught her eye. *The friendship bracelet.* "You still have it?" She tenderly touched the woven strands.

"Of course. I put it back on yesterday. And I don't plan to take it off again."

She hadn't noticed it last night, either distracted by the glitz of the gala or his suit jacket had kept it hidden. She smiled softly, wondering whatever happened to the one she'd made for Kevin. "It looks good on you."

"There's something I need to tell you. About this bracelet. About the night Kevin died." His voice strained, and sadness glinted in his eyes.

"What is it?" Is it what he'd wanted to tell her last night before their argument?

"First, how about we take *Mira* out for a spin?"

"Is she seaworthy?"

"Yep. I checked with Mackensie and did a thorough inspection myself." He held out his hand. "So, what d'ya say? Will you be my first mate?"

Cap wiggled by his side, eager to climb aboard.

"I thought you'd never ask." Sage slid her hand in Flynn's. His firm, assured grasp closed over hers.

With Flynn, she'd willingly go wherever the wind took them. But she couldn't quiet a faint whisper of restless curiosity.

What did he need to tell her?

Chapter 39

FLYNN

FLYNN TILTED his face toward the sun, relishing the wind and salty spray as *Mira* sailed across the frosty-tipped water. He breathed in the invigorating, tangy scent of the sea that also smelled deliciously sweet, like hope and second chances.

By his side, Cap stuck his snout into the air, his tongue flopping to one side as the wind ruffled his golden mane.

"What d'ya think, bud? You like the seafaring life?"

Cap barked his approval, and Flynn laughed.

It had been years since he'd sailed, but it all came rushing back in a flurry—exhilarating and freeing, as if the great blue expanse went on forever.

He glanced at Sage standing near the bow. With her honey-colored curls fluttering around her slender neck and shoulders, and her long, gauzy dress billowing around her perfect frame, she looked like a sea nymph or siren—stunning, ethereal, and almost *too* alluring. In her presence, he found it difficult to concentrate. Thankfully, the sailing conditions couldn't be smoother, and Mackensie had custom-built *Mira* to require as few hands on deck as possible.

Plus, just like old times, Sage proved to be an excellent first mate, further solidifying in his heart that, together, there wasn't anything they couldn't accomplish.

They followed the coastline, heading north toward the Tanti Islands, daydreaming about bookish sailing tours and what the future held. For a moment in time, they existed in a perfect bubble of bliss, unmarred by heartache and loss.

He was tempted to keep sailing and never look back.

The mirthful mood shifted as they rounded a craggy sea stack and Coyote Cave came into view. Goose bumps pricked his arms.

Sage met his gaze, her eyes troubled and questioning. Almost immediately, her expression softened, as if she understood, at least on some level, that he needed to do this—he needed to face the past.

The cave, carved into a rocky promontory, garnered its name from the prolific coyote mint plant that covered the cliffside in fragrant, lavender-hued blooms. It used to be a favorite local haunt until Kevin's accident. Now, a battered chain-link fence guarded the entrance.

As if in reverence of that fateful day, the sun dipped behind a cloud, casting shadows on the headland. His stomach clenched as they drew closer.

Speaking only when needed, they worked in tandem, anchoring *Mira* offshore.

While they completed the necessary tasks, trepidation built in Flynn's chest. He hadn't been back to the cave since the night of Kevin's memorial service. He could still feel the heat of a hundred or more votive candles illuminating the beach, flickering across the inky-black water. His parents had wanted him to speak that night, to say something in remembrance of his brother. But he hadn't been able to form a single word past the guilt and regret strangling his throat.

Wordlessly, Flynn helped Sage and Cap into the inflatable kayak. They paddled in silence, both lost in their thoughts.

Before they made it all the way to shore, Cap bounded into the shallow waves, prancing in the surf, oblivious to the significance of their excursion.

They beached the kayak, and Flynn hopped onto the wet sand. Sage followed. Together, they dragged the kayak onto the berm, safe from the rising tide.

The wind echoed ominously in the small cove, and frothy waves thrashed against the rocks surrounding the cave. An eerie feeling crept over him. Was coming here a mistake?

"Are you okay?" Sage touched his arm gently, yanking him from his thoughts.

"Are you?" He realized bringing her here conjured her own ghosts and painful memories.

"Honestly? I never expected to come back here."

"Me, neither," he admitted, noticing neither of them had actually answered the question. "But there's something I need to do." He twisted the bracelet around his wrist. "Right before graduation, Kev got this crazy idea to make a time capsule. One of his business gurus recommended it. He said to include a letter to our future selves and an item that represented something important in our lives. The plan was to open it in ten years, after we'd become roaring successes, to remind us what really matters."

"That sounds like Kevin." Sage smiled wistfully. "And you buried it here?"

"Kev did. In the cave." His throat went dry.

Her eyes widened. "You're going inside?"

"Assuming it's still there, it'll only take me a minute to find it." He knew exactly where Kev hid it—in a crescent-shaped crevice near the back of the cave, to the left of a chipped stalactite.

"I'm coming with you." Her words carried conviction, but he caught the glint of dismay in her eyes.

He appreciated her willingness, but this was something he needed to do alone. "Keep an eye on Cap. If he keeps rolling around in the wet sand like that, we'll wind up taking half the beach back with us."

She reached for his hand, gripping tightly as she held his gaze. How did she communicate so much love and support in a single glance?

He kissed her softly, sinking into her lips, savoring their sweetness and assurance.

The sun slid from behind the clouds, momentarily lending its comforting light.

Before he pulled away, he pressed his forehead to hers for a fraction of a second, gathering strength from her presence. He straightened, forcing a smile. "I'll be back in a jiffy."

"I'll be here."

He felt her concerned gaze on his back as he ambled across the sandy shore, up the rocky embankment, and over the rickety fence, weatherbeaten by the wind and waves. The rusty chain links clanged as he hoisted himself over the side. He landed with a splash in ankle-deep water, grateful his deck shoes could handle getting wet.

The frigid water rose to his calves, then up to his thighs as he made his way farther into the cave. Dank, gloomy walls held in the darkness, save for faint shafts of light streaming through the narrow entrance, softening the shadows.

Flynn kept his gaze fixed straight ahead, fighting a barrage of unwelcome images—images of his brother that haunted his nightmares.

His foot slipped, and he dunked waist-deep into the water. Shocked by the cold, he inhaled sharply, filling his lungs with the scent of salt and sediment. The oppressive air crowded around him, covering him like a damp cloak, forcing him deeper into the murky depths.

He squinted into the blackness up ahead, barely making out the half-moon outline. The crevice. He was almost there. *You can do this.*

His breaths came in shallow gasps as he pressed onward, the silty ground giving way, forcing him to swim. After what felt like two lifetimes—but probably lasted only two minutes—he reached the far end of the cave. He ran his hands along the slippery surface, searching for a place to grab hold. Locating a groove that would give him the necessary leverage, he hauled himself far enough out of the water to reach a hand into the crescent-shaped slit in the slab of earth.

One by one, he removed the stones Kevin had used as a protective barrier, scraping and scooping out sand and pebbles until his fingertips met something slick and smooth.

The trinket box! It was still there. Relief surged through him. Kev would be pleased the box had lived up to the advertising hype—and the hefty price tag.

Okay, time to go.

He tried to withdraw his hand, but it didn't budge. The friendship bracelet snagged on something sharp, pinning his arm in place. In the span of a single ragged breath, fear and adrenaline pumped into his bloodstream. His pulse pounded in his eardrums, drowning out the cacophonous crash of ocean waves.

Suddenly, all the visions he'd kept at bay came barreling into his thoughts.

Visions of Kevin trapped and alone, the tide rising, flooding the cave as he called for help that never came.

Called for him....

His chest constricted with a piercing stab of pain.

As he yanked and twisted in a blind panic, the bracelet dislodged, along with the box, and the unexpected shift sent him backward, plunging into the dark pool. Fully submerged, the icy surface closed over him like a frosted blanket, biting and abrasive. Clutching the box, he resurfaced, choking on salt water and a sob buried deep in his throat—deep in his soul, where it clawed to get out.

By the time he made it back to the beach, he couldn't contain his tears.

He collapsed in the sand and let them fall, blurring Sage's outline as she knelt beside him, gathering him in her arms.

Chapter 40

FLYNN

FLYNN SCRUBBED HIS DAMP FACE, drying the tears. If it had been anyone else but Sage on that beach, he would've been embarrassed by the outpouring of pent-up emotion. But part of him appreciated the ability to be vulnerable with someone who understood his grief. At least, partially understood. He still hadn't told her the whole story.

"I'm so sorry," she whispered, stroking his hand as they sat side by side in the sand. "It must have been awful." Her voice carried on a tentative breath, as if she couldn't even imagine what he'd experienced.

She sat so close he felt the heat radiating off her body. She didn't seem to mind his wet clothes and hair soaking her own as she sat pressed up against him, her head bent toward his.

Cap didn't seem to mind, either. The compassionate pup nestled his muzzle in Flynn's lap, gazing up at him with comforting big brown eyes.

Flynn scratched the scruff at his neck, letting him know everything would be okay. *Eventually.*

"Are you going to open it?" Sage asked softly, casting a

timid glance at the time capsule resting in the sand beside him.

"Yes, but there's something I need to tell you first." A tremor of foreboding traveled through him, scattering goose bumps across his skin. He didn't want to open this particular wound to the harsh light of day. But if he didn't, he knew it would never heal.

"What is it?" She threaded her fingers through his and folded them closed, clasping his hand in a tender, reassuring hold.

"The night Kevin died—" His throat constricted around the words, raw and swollen. The backs of his eyes stung. *Come on. Keep going.*

He gulped air, forcing himself to continue. "The night Kevin died, I was supposed to be with him. We agreed to meet at the cave before high tide. I was supposed to bring my letter and the item I'd chosen, and then we'd bury the time capsule together. Only, I never showed."

The confession burned like acid, and it hurt to swallow. He pictured his brother waiting for him as the hours ticked by, the tide getting higher by the minute.

He felt Sage's gaze but couldn't bring himself to look at her. He couldn't bear to see disapproval and disappointment in her eyes. *Once again, he'd left someone hanging.*

Instead, he stared straight out to sea, watching a bird dip its wings in the water. "I'd planned to be there. But that morning, you texted, asking to get together that afternoon to go over a new route for our post-graduation sailing adventure. I knew it was cutting it close, but I thought I could hang out with you, then meet up with Kevin afterward." A sad, sardonic smile tugged the corner of his mouth. "Except,

I should've known better. With you, I always lost track of time. And—" A fresh surge of grief grabbed hold of his heart, gripping tightly.

He squeezed his eyes shut, forbidding the tears from falling.

Sage pressed her fingertips against the back of his hand, firm yet gentle, encouraging him to go on.

"When I finally checked the time, I realized I'd never make it, so I decided I'd stay with you and apologize to Kevin later. I figured he'd get bored waiting around for me, go home, and we could try again the next day." Shame coated his words, thick and rough so they scraped his throat on the way out.

"I didn't even call, counting on an apology later to smooth things over. But I never got the chance." Blinking, he glanced up at the sky. Puffy white clouds dotted a blanket of blue, looking down on him, passing judgment. Judgment he deserved. "Kevin went into the cave at high tide because he'd wasted time waiting for me. If I'd been there like I'd promised, he would still be here."

Anger and self-loathing sat in his stomach like a smoldering coal. A reminder he carried with him, eternally stoked by his regret.

"There's no way you can know that for sure." Her tone was kind and gentle, but he heard the quiver of pain. And it pierced right through him.

"I can be pretty darn certain," he said bitterly. "If I wasn't such a selfish jerk, my brother would still be alive." Pressure built in his chest, making it hard to breathe. "*This*," he rasped, "is why I've devoted my life to achieving all the things Kevin couldn't. Because of me, he never had the chance."

The horizon line blurred, becoming a jumble of muted blues. He thought of how he'd given Sage *Mira* and turned down the promotion. Was he being selfish again? What would Kevin want him to do?

As if she could read his thoughts, Sage gave his hand the kind of squeeze that said, *You'd better listen up.* "What happened to Kevin was an accident. A horrible, tragic, heartbreaking accident. I know you miss him. So do I. But you loved Kevin. Fiercely. You'd do anything for him. And he knew that, without a doubt. One decision you made at eighteen doesn't change the bond you two had or how much you loved him. Or how much he loved you."

Her words tore into his heart like a rigging knife, ripping away the tattered seams of a wind-beaten sail so they could finally be repaired.

He forced himself to meet her gaze, broken anew by the unconditional love reflected in her glistening sea-green eyes.

"Kevin wouldn't want you to live his life," she said, her voice soft and trembling. "He'd want you to live yours. He was so proud of you, Flynn. He always said people like him ran the world. But people like you were the ones who knew how to *live* in it."

A surge of warmth washed over him, as real and tangible as the sun's rays. Had his brother really felt that way?

Sage leaned closer, as if to ensure he didn't miss a single word she said. "Kevin may have cared a lot about making money and a name for himself, but he cared about *you* more."

Cap wiggled in the sand beside him as if he wholeheartedly agreed.

Flynn let her words sink in, and the tightness in his chest

released, like a pressure valve being opened. "How'd you get so wise?" he teased, using levity to ease his mounting emotions.

"Must be all the books I read." She smiled through her tears.

The wind tossed her curls around her face. A few strands stuck to her tearstained cheeks, and her nose glowed a pinkish red. But she'd never looked more beautiful.

She's the greatest blessing in your life. And you'd better do everything in your power to show her that every day, in as many ways as possible.

He reached for the time capsule, ready to face whatever he found inside.

Heart thrumming, he entered the code in the manual lock—their birthdate, which was easy to remember.

As he flipped open the lid, he broke into a grin.

Great minds think alike.

A blue and white friendship bracelet rested inside.

Sage gasped, her entire face beaming like the sun hanging low in the sky before them. She scooted closer, tears shimmering in her eyes as he lifted the letter.

A sheet of white paper, neatly folded into a symmetrical square.

He carefully smoothed out the creases.

A single word stared back at them from the center of the page.

Family.

A lump lodged in his throat.

Here come the waterworks again.

"Well," he said with a raspy chuckle. "He gets bonus points for brevity."

Sage laughed, light and lilting—the most captivating, cleansing sound.

He slipped an arm around her shoulders, one hand petting Cap, as the sun dipped toward the horizon line, splashing pinks and gold across the waves.

Although he sat anchored on shore, not sailing across the sea with the wind at his back, he'd never felt freer.

Chapter 41

ABBY

STANDING AT *MIRA*'S BOW, Abby gazed across the sun-soaked water. The gilded circle sank into the horizon, diffusing in every direction like fresh-churned butter melting over the surface.

Music and laughter mingled with the melody of ocean waves, and Abby tore her gaze from the mesmerizing view to take in an even more glorious sight. The joyous tableau of her loved ones gathered on deck to celebrate The Unbound Bookshop's inaugural sunset sail. Logan, Max, Verna, Nadia, Evan, and so many others she loved and cherished sipped strawberry lemonade, alternating their awestruck attention between the sun's stunning watercolor display and the rugged coastline drenched in gold.

More than three weeks had passed since Sage announced her new business venture with Flynn—and their rekindled relationship. Abby had never seen her friend happier. Flynn had given up his promotion altogether, and they'd spent every waking moment transforming *Mira*'s interior into a bookish wonderland. While the renovations weren't yet completed, they'd managed to stock the shelves with enough books to open for business. A soft opening, at least. Abby knew it was only the beginning, and she couldn't wait to see how their dream unfolded.

Tonight, Flynn stood at the wheel—or was it called the helm? He wore a white captain's hat, skewed to one side as if he didn't take himself too seriously. Sage leaned against him, tucked under his arm, her expression the epitome of blissful contentment.

A similar feeling of happiness—warm, airy, and light—spread through Abby, teasing her lips into a smile. And she felt something else, too, something deeper. A gratitude that extended into the very core of her being, grounding her in the present while her thoughts roamed free, daydreaming about the future.

A dog's bark drew her attention toward the back of the boat where Max played tug-of-war with Cap and a scrap of old rope. Her heart swelled with motherly affection. He may not be hers forever, but she'd cherish however long they had together, praying and hoping it would last. And with Logan by her side, they'd give him all the love they possessed and the sense of family and belonging he needed.

Her thoughts shifted to Logan. Where was he? He was with Max a moment ago....

"Pretty incredible, isn't it?" Logan appeared by her side, nodding toward the horizon. With the sun settled in for the night, twilight painted the sky in silvery shades of blue.

"Gorgeous," she murmured, her voice soft and reverent as a seagull soared low above the water, graceful and serene.

"Granted, it doesn't beat hitting Mach 2 at forty thousand

feet, but I could get used to this sailing thing." Standing at her back, Logan draped his arms around her shoulders, hugging her from behind. She leaned her head against his chest, snuggling deeper into his embrace, enveloped by his comforting scent.

Would there ever be a moment more perfect than this?

Maybe when Logan proposes. She felt a tiny twinge of disappointment at the thought, but immediately shoved it aside. The evening was far too wonderful to taint with her impatience.

Logan would propose when he wanted. She could wait.

But no matter how hard she tried, she couldn't stop thinking about the sugar bowl. The more she thought about the moment he'd surprised her with the thoughtful gift, the more convinced she became that Logan had been about to propose that day.

At first, she wondered if he'd try again once Piper moved out. But it had been two weeks since she'd rented the old gray house at the end of State Street. And almost three since she'd started her new job at the Sawmill. Piper had turned the page to the next chapter in her life, and Abby was genuinely pleased for her.

But when would her next chapter begin?

Wind whipped salty spray over the bow as *Mira* rounded a rocky headland, steering back toward town. The old lighthouse greeted them from the tip of the cape.

"Look!" Her heart soared as a familiar shape came into view. The inn sat high on the bluff, overlooking the bay. Soft light shone through the windows, warm and inviting, welcoming them home. "Have you ever seen anything more beautiful?"

"You haven't even seen the best part yet," Logan told her, his tone strangely husky.

As they drew closer, Abby could make out strands of white twinkle lights decorating the stone wall perimeter surrounding their backyard.

Her pulse fluttered in her throat.

Was that—?

She blinked, worried her eyes were playing tricks on her. Maybe in her eagerness, she'd conjured the whole thing in her mind?

Even after her double take, the glittering lights spelled the same unmistakable message.

Marry Me?

Stunned, she turned in Logan's arms to face him.

He dropped to one knee, there on the deck, with all their friends watching.

"Abigail Preston." Holding her gaze, he pulled a tiny velvet bag from his back pocket. "Before I met you, I went through life without a real purpose, nursing my wounds, resigned to an empty existence. But you helped me see that God doesn't leave us in our brokenness. He can take even the rustiest, worn-down, battered parts of ourselves that we try to hide from the world and use them for something good."

Logan's voice cracked with emotion, and Abby clasped her hands tightly together to keep from throwing herself into his arms before he'd had a chance to finish.

"He also gives us good things, even when we don't deserve them. Like how He gave me you. The greatest blessing I could ever ask for." Logan tugged on the thin cord tying the velvet bag closed.

Her heart beat so quickly, it seemed to stop altogether, the way a hummingbird hovered in place.

Logan withdrew a square-cut diamond set in a white gold band—exquisite in its simplicity. "This was my mother's. I never thought of myself as the kind of guy to give someone a hand-me-down ring. I guess it always seemed kinda cheesy. But I get it now." His intense gaze glinted with the sheen of unshed tears. "My mother's ring makes me think of home. Of happy memories. Of the love my parents shared. The love that made us a family. Now, *you're* my family. And you've made our house a home."

He held the ring aloft.

Abby's breath hitched. *This was it.* The moment she'd longed for, day and night. Only, it surpassed even her most elaborate daydreams.

"Before you, I had nothing. Now, I have everything. And as long as you don't have any objections, I'd like to spend the rest of my life showing you just how grateful I am." He cracked a slow, sexy smile, and Abby barely refrained from collapsing straight into his arms. "Does that sound okay to you?" he prompted, still flashing the most adorable, endearing grin.

"I think I could learn to live with that." She grinned back, so overcome with joy, she practically floated in midair.

Logan slid the ring onto her finger, then scooped her into his arms.

Amid celebratory cheers, he captured her lips in a kiss that brought the past, present, and future into one crystal-clear moment where time didn't exist.

She'd just promised him forever. But even forever didn't feel like long enough.

When their lips finally parted, their loved ones gathered around them to offer their congratulations. Max raced to give them both a hug, and as they huddled in a family embrace, her thoughts flickered to the sliver of orange sea glass encased in a glass jar on her nightstand.

Moved by love and gratitude, her heart whispered a silent prayer.

A prayer she'd repeat all the days of her life.

Thank you for the deep waters that brought me to this blessing.

And all the blessings yet to come.

CECE

CeCe Dupree sipped her lemonade, smiling at the evening's events. Abby and Logan engaged. Sage and Flynn embarking on a grand new adventure. Even Sage's mom found someone.

"Love is in the air tonight, isn't it?" Janet Hill sidled up to CeCe at the stern and sniffed, as if she could actually smell something other than the ocean.

"For some people." CeCe hoped she sounded nonchalant, not bitter. She didn't begrudge anyone else's happiness just because her own romantic life smelled more like moldy sourdough than whatever sweet scent Janet detected.

"It could be your lucky night, too, you know." Janet's heavily lined eyes sparkled. Behind her, the warm glow of Main Street illuminated the bluff, twinkling in tandem with the pale stars studding the lavender-gray sky.

"What do you mean?" Wary, CeCe took another sip of lemonade. Of all the meddling albeit well-meaning Belles, Janet Hill was the wild card. You never knew what she had up her sleeve.

"I want to set you up with my nephew Owen."

CeCe suppressed an internal groan. *Not another setup.*

"He's a catch," Janet insisted. "And you two have a lot in common."

"Oh? Like what?" CeCe asked, humoring her.

"He works in a bakery."

"Really?" *Huh.* That was new. No one had set her up with another baker before. Maybe he had potential?

"Technically, he's an accountant for a bakery chain," Janet corrected, quickly adding, "But he's a pastry connoisseur. And he looks like a young Robert Taylor."

"Who?"

Janet rolled her eyes, clearly exasperated with her ignorance. "Never mind. Owen is a hunk. And he knows the difference between a baguette and a brioche. What more could a girl want?"

An image of her childhood crush, Jayce Hunt, flickered in CeCe's mind. His dark, unruly hair that he could never fully tame, no matter how many expensive gels he tried. The tiny dent near the corner of his mouth. Not quite a dimple, but close—and distractingly adorable. Since kindergarten, no other boy could compare. But he'd never view her as anything more than his nerdy, flour-covered best friend.

As if he'd read her mind from hundreds of miles away, her phone warbled his personalized ringtone. Her heart skipped, then stumbled, like it always did whenever he called. "Excuse me, Janet. I should take this."

"Okay, but think about what I said. You and Owen would make a fabulous couple."

"I will," she promised, already pulling her cell from the crossbody clutch slung over her shoulder. Scooting toward the railing, she answered the call. "Hey, what are you doing awake?" she asked in lieu of a greeting. "Isn't it like 5 a.m. in Paris?"

"Like you always say, the best time to buy baked goods is first thing in the morning." His voice scratched with an early morning rasp, as if he'd just woken up, and the sultry sound gave her goose bumps.

Get a grip, CeCe.

"I'm buying pastries for the crew," he explained. "And I can't remember what you said I should try? They're like doughnut holes?"

Of course he was buying pastries for the crew. Such a sweet Jayce-like thing to do. Even as one of Hollywood's hottest heartthrobs, who was filming a new rom-com in Paris, he hadn't lost his boy-next-door charm.

"Chouquettes," she said with her mother's Caribbean-French accent. Although she made the light, fluffy pastries sprinkled with crunchy pearl sugar at her own bakery, she could appreciate the pleasure of enjoying them in Paris.

They would taste even sweeter with Jayce. She shook away the thought.

"Riiiiight. Chouquette," he said, pronouncing *shoo-ket* clumsily.

She smiled to herself. *You gotta love a man for trying.*

Ugh. She loved him too much. That was the problem. *You're friends, nothing more. Get it through your thick head already.*

"Thanks," he said casually. She pictured him strolling the cobbled Parisian streets, onlookers gawking as they recognized his chiseled jawline and midnight-blue eyes. "What are you up to?"

"Sailing around the bay."

"Uh-huh," he scoffed. "And I'm bungee jumping off the Eiffel Tower."

"I'm serious. I'm on a sunset cruise. It's beautiful." She felt a little miffed. Okay, so she was a homebody who spent most evenings curled up on the couch with a book or TV show and her cantankerous cat. But was it so hard to believe she could be doing something interesting for a change?

"Are you on a date or something?"

Did she detect a hit of jealousy in his inflection? *No.* That would be crazy.

"Would I answer the phone if I was on a date?"

"For me? Your very best friend in the whole world? Yes. Always." She could tell from his tone that he was teasing, but he had no idea how right he was.

"Hey, guess what?" he asked suddenly.

"What?"

"I'm coming home before the press tour starts. And I have a favor to ask you."

"A favor? What kind of favor?"

"A big one. But—" He paused to say something in stilted French to someone on the other end of the phone. "Hey, Toto," he said, using the nickname he'd given her in third grade, "I gotta go. I'm at the bakery and running late to set, but I'll call you in a few days, okay?"

"Okay." She didn't want to hang up. She missed his voice. She missed *him*.

"I'll bring you back some real French macarons to butter you up. One taste and you won't be able to say no." There was more jostling of the phone followed by a rushed goodbye.

She stared at the blank screen.

Jayce was coming home soon.

And he wanted to ask her for a favor.

A *big* one, he'd said. And he'd sounded serious.

How big of a favor could it be?

Discover Jayce's big favor (and follow CeCe, Abby, Logan, Max, and our other friends in Blessings Bay) in **The Uncomplicated Café.**

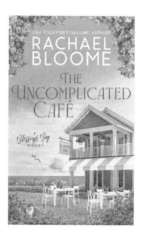

Is happily ever after more simple than it seems?

Acknowledgments

Here we are again. The release of The Unbound Bookshop marks a dozen books. Can you believe it?

With each book, I'm more and more grateful for all the overwhelming help and support I've received over the years.

I wonder if my husband knew what he was getting into when I said, "Hey, I think I have an idea for a Christmas book," back in December of 2018. Since then, he's been by my side, championing me—and keeping me caffeinated—through the publication of twelve books. He's nothing short of heroic.

I'd also like to thank my incredible family, who continues to support me, even when I blatantly steal details from their lives to include in my novels. I love you guys.

Of course, I can't forget Gwenn—the woman who inspired it all. I'm grateful for her inspiration, her testimony, her prayers, and her friendship. She and her husband, Glenn, came to visit us in California earlier this year, further cementing their special place in my heart. It was incredibly hard to say goodbye! They are the very definition of found family, and if you ever get the chance to meet them, you'll understand what I mean.

In fact, you should do yourself a favor right now and book your stay at blessingsonstate.com. You'll thank me later!

I also owe an eternal debt of gratitude to Ana Grigoriu-Voicu with Books-Design, who continues to outdo herself with each cover, Krista Dapkey with KD Proofreading, for her brilliant editing skills and endless patience, and Beth Attwood, for her impeccable proofing skills that add the extra polish and shine. These ladies are a powerhouse of talent, and I'm so thankful to have them on my team.

Continued thanks to Dave Cenker, for his friendship that carries through even the more challenging writerly seasons. And to Dawn Malone and Elizabeth Bråten—I've loved getting to know you ladies. You inspire me with your beautiful writing and kind hearts, and I look forward to growing our craft and businesses together.

Hugs and heartfelt thanks to my fabulous ARC Team, who tirelessly catch the pesky typos I miss even after reading the book a hundred times.

And thank you to all the truly amazing readers in the Secret Garden Book Club, my favorite corner of Facebook. You guys make me smile. I wish we could all grab coffee together!

And lastly, to every reader who has ever read one of my books—thank you! You help keep the lights on. But seriously, you make this dream-turned-career possible. And I will forever be grateful.

About the Author

Rachael Bloome is a *USA Today* bestselling author of contemporary romance and women's fiction novels featuring hope, healing, and the unbreakable bonds of found family.

Rachael is a hope*ful* romantic joyfully living in her very own love story. She's passionate about her faith, family, friends, and her French press. When she's not writing, helping to run the family coffee roasting business, or getting together with friends, she's busy planning their next big adventure.

Learn more about Rachael and her uplifting love stories at www.rachaelbloome.com and connect via the following social media sites (you can even listen to free audiobooks on her YouTube channel!):

Abby's Celebration Waffles Recipe

INGREDIENTS

3 eggs

1 cup milk

1 cup vanilla Greek yogurt (or lemon for extra lemon flavor)

2 teaspoons vanilla extract

¼ lemon zest (optional)

2 tablespoons butter, melted

2 cups all-purpose flour

¼ cup sugar

2 teaspoons baking powder

¼ teaspoon salt

¼ cup sprinkles, plus more for decorating

INSTRUCTIONS

Separate the egg yolks and egg whites. Whip egg whites until frothy.

In a large mixing bowl, whisk the egg yolks, milk, yogurt, vanilla, lemon zest, and butter until smooth.

In a separate bowl, combine the flour, baking powder, sugar, and salt.

Add the dry ingredients to the wet ingredients and mix until the batter is smooth, not lumpy, being careful not to overmix.

Gently fold in the egg whites and sprinkles.

Lightly grease a preheated waffle maker with butter.

Pour enough batter to nearly fill the bottom plate.

Cook the waffle on your preferred setting or until the exterior is golden brown.

Repeat with the remaining batter.

Top with your preferred toppings. Homemade whipped cream with additional sprinkles and/or lemon zest is a favorite. Additional options include but are not limited to: butter, maple syrup, powdered sugar, fresh berries, berry jam or compote, and lemon curd.

Serve warm and enjoy!

Book Club Questions

1. Which character did you identify with the most? And why?

2. What did you think of the way Abby handled the situation with Piper? What would you have done differently?

3. Were you surprised by the paternity test results? Do you think Abby should forgive Donnie for the affair? Why or why not?

4. Our life experiences can greatly impact the choices we make, and both Sage and Flynn struggled with misconceptions formed by painful situations in their pasts. In what ways did you see them grow over the course of the story?

5. After the death of Flynn's brother, Flynn and his parents grieved in different ways. What advice would you give to each of them to help with the healing process?

6. Verna tells Abby that forgiveness isn't a weakness, it's a sign of great strength. Do you agree? Why or why not?

7. Do you think Flynn should feel guilty over what happened to his brother? Why or why not?

8. What do you think of Sage and Flynn's new business venture? If The Unbound Bookshop really existed, would you like to visit?

9. Sage felt a stronger connection to Flynn when she discovered he'd read her favorite book. Why do you think she reacted that way? Do you think books have the ability to connect people on a deeper level? Why or why not?

10. Grandma Shirley tells Sage that being single is a blessing for many reasons, but so is finding your person and going through life together as a team. Do you agree with this statement? How would

you describe the blessings of being single versus the blessings of being married?

11. If you had to create a time capsule similar to the one Flynn's brother made, what would your letter say? And what item would you choose to include?

12. What do you think is the main theme of the novel? And why?

As always, I look forward to hearing your thoughts on the story. You can email your responses (or ask your own questions) at hello@rachaelbloome.com or post them in my private Facebook group, Rachael Bloome's Secret Garden Book Club.

Also by Rachael Bloome

Rachael Bloome
STORIES WITH HEART & HOPE

POPPY CREEK SERIES

The Clause in Christmas

The Truth in Tiramisu

The Secret in Sandcastles

The Meaning in Mistletoe

The Faith in Flowers

The Whisper in Wind

The Hope in Hot Chocolate

The Promise in Poppies

A Very Barrie Christmas

STANDALONE NOVELS

New York, New Year, New You

Made in United States
North Haven, CT
10 March 2025

66641782R00171